THE FOREST
IN THE
HALLWAY

by GORDON SMITH

CLARION BOOKS

NEW YORK

Clarion Books
a Houghton Mifflin Company imprint
215 Park Avenue South, New York, NY 10003
Copyright © 2006 by Gordon Smith

The text was set in 12-point Bembo.
Design by Michelle Gengaro-Kokmen.

www.clarionbooks.com

Printed in the U.S.A.

Library of Congress Cataloging-in-Publication Data

Smith, Gordon R., 1951–
The forest in the hallway / by Gordon Smith.
p.   cm.
Summary: Accompanied by a mysterious lost boy and a rowdy family
with strange powers, fourteen-year-old Beatriz searches for her missing
parents while evading a band of slave traders and a vengeful witch.
ISBN-13: 978-0-618-68847-0
ISBN-10: 0-618-68847-1
[1. Magic—Fiction. 2. Parents—Fiction. 3. Witches—Fiction.] I. Title.
PZ7.S64862 For 2006
[Fic]—dc22   2006015659

HAD   10 9 8 7 6 5 4 3 2 1

For Holly, Georgia, and Andrea

THE FOREST
IN THE
HALLWAY

1

NEW YORK

BEATRIZ SAT ON A WINDOW SEAT overlooking the rainy New York City streets, stroking her uncle's cat and wondering if she ought to brush its hair off her sweat-shirt. Again. Raindrops made their way hesitantly down the cool glass panes, and the trees in the park across the street waved wildly in the wind, frozen in position occasionally by flashes of lightning.

She was bored. The air conditoning was too cold. And she was filled with an overwhelming sense of dread. It was a weight in her stomach, heavy as a stone.

Two weeks ago she had been home in Des Moines, Iowa. And two weeks ago, on a hot July afternoon, her mother and father had mysteriously disappeared—just vanished—on the day before her fourteenth birthday.

She had tried calling her mother's cell phone. It rang in her purse, in the hall closet. Her mother never went anywhere without her purse. She waited until nine thirty before calling Holly, her best friend. Twenty minutes later, Holly and her parents arrived and reassured Beatriz that everything was fine, there must have been a mix-up, and had her folks said anything about going out tonight?

An hour later, after Holly's dad had looked through every room in the house and her mom had made half a dozen phone calls, the grownups had a quiet talk and told Beatriz they were going to call the police, "just as a precaution."

From the half of it she could hear, the conversation with the police seemed to Beatriz extremely brief and casual. When it was over, Holly's mom told Beatriz that the police had asked them to leave a note and take her home with them for the night. "They said to call in the morning if your mom and dad still haven't come back."

Haven't come back? How could they not come back?

She lay in bed the next morning, having not slept much, and stared at the ceiling. Where were they? They'd never done anything even remotely like this before.

"Beatriz?" Holly's mother knocked softly. "Can you get up now? They want us to go down to the police station."

She was interviewed by a patient and sympathetic policewoman in a gray, windowless room, and shown photographs in big loose-leaf binders—photographs of scary-looking men with lifeless eyes. She'd never seen any of them. Did the police think one of these men had done something to her parents?

After driving home for a rather somber lunch, Holly's mother took Beatriz back to her house to get fresh clothes, explaining in the car that they'd be meeting the policewoman there. Beatriz felt a little as if she had been tricked into this. She didn't want to talk to the police again. Why did they have to be at her house? Why weren't they looking for her mom and dad?

The policewoman and Holly's mom walked her through the house to see if anything seemed odd or out of place. Only one thing seemed strange: There was a wide gap in the top shelf of her father's books—strange, because he always put his books back or moved the bookend down to keep the row neat. She had no idea what was missing.

The policewoman asked for a picture of her parents, and Beatriz broke into tears when she couldn't find one. Where was the big box of photographs? Why hadn't her parents ever organized them into albums?

There were three messages on the answering machine. Two from yesterday (the dentist and someone from her mother's book group) and one from today: her uncle M—her father's brother—calling to wish her a happy birthday. The officer said the messages didn't seem particularly helpful, but could she take the tape with her to the station anyway? She also asked for Uncle M's phone number, which Beatriz was able to find.

Riding back in the car to Holly's house, Beatriz stared straight ahead, silent. Holly's mother glanced over at her every so often but didn't speak, either.

Beatriz stayed at Holly's house for a week, waiting, but none of the phone calls from the police had anything positive to report, and her parents didn't come back.

On the eighth day, Holly's mother, while braiding Holly's long brown hair, gently announced to Beatriz that her uncle had offered to let her stay with him in New York City until her parents were located. She'd rather Beatriz stay with them, of course, but it would be too complicated, what with Holly's grandparents coming to visit for three weeks. There just wasn't enough room.

Beatriz stared at her hands and said nothing.

Four days later she found herself in an unfamiliar apartment with a man she knew mainly from his annual birthday phone call and his Christmas cards. Despite the fact that he and Beatriz's father were twin brothers—or perhaps because of it—they weren't all that close. Her family had only once gone to see him in New York—when she was six—and she couldn't remember him ever visiting Des Moines. She had seen him a second time at a relative's funeral, a few years ago. He gave her a cheese sandwich and a conspiratorial look that seemed to say he couldn't stand being there, either.

Now he paced back and forth in the living room like a bewildered Sherlock Holmes. There hadn't been any news since her arrival. "Honestly, my dear, if there was anything, good or bad, I'd tell you."

Bad news? She bit her lip. He wasn't very good at being comforting. *Maybe it's because he never had children of his own.* There had been a divorce, her mother said, when Beatriz was a baby.

This was so much worse than waiting for her parents at Holly's house. Why couldn't she have stayed there? They could have put up a tent in the backyard.

She kept out of her uncle's way, spending much of her time sitting on the bed in the guest room, knees pulled up close to her chest, running through what was by now a fixed set of scenarios of what might have happened. All of them were dreadful.

When her uncle went out, which he did frequently but at odd times *(Doesn't he have a job?),* she wandered around the apartment, looking at his things. There were lots of souvenirs from Asia, where he'd apparently spent a good deal of time. He had statues and drawings and books in Chinese, Korean, and Russian; beautiful Indian carpets; and prints of snow scenes in rural Japan.

On his mantelpiece he kept a framed photograph of a beautiful young woman: his grandmother, for whom Beatriz had been named, who had emigrated from Portugal in the 1800s.

He also had a large collection of leather-bound books on witchcraft. They were locked in a glass-fronted bookcase, and he said he would bring some of them out for her to look at one of these days. But after being put off several times, Beatriz realized he didn't really want to show them to her, so she stopped asking.

The apartment was pleasant during the day, but the nights were awful. Beatriz hated going to bed. Her room was dark and scary. Light from the street filtered up through the sycamore trees in front of the building and made scratchy, branchy shadows on the ceiling. There was a blue neon HOTEL sign on top of another building a few blocks away that flashed faintly on one of her walls. You would hardly notice it unless you looked for it, but of course she always did.

She missed the warm light from the kitchen at home that trickled around the hall corner into her room, and the sound of her parents talking and doing the dishes after she went to bed. She especially missed them looking in on her on their way upstairs.

So she was bored, in addition to being miserable, sitting in the living-room window seat and gazing out at the late-afternoon storm, when she noticed a face in the grain of the wood of the window sash. This is nothing unusual; an idle mind looking for distraction can see faces in clouds or bathroom tiles or ceiling cracks or in any number of places. But this face moved. It winked. Beatriz stared at the two little knots that were its eyes and tried not to blink. When, after a few seconds, nothing happened, she began to doubt she had seen anything at all. Then it winked again, and a hoarse whisper came from a small crack below the knots. "Nineteenth floor! Everybody out! Home Furnishings, Lost and Found—going down!"

Beatriz frowned.

She watched it for several minutes more before it

hissed, "Nineteenth floor, stupid! Numero Nineteen-o! One-Niner, Houston, do you copy? Helloooo, Mama!" After that the eyes flipped shut and did not reopen.

Hello, Mama?

2
THE FOREST

HER UNCLE'S APARTMENT BUILDING was in an older section of Manhattan. Made of rough gray granite blocks, it rose nineteen stories above the tree-lined sidewalk. The lobby was very clean and very quiet, furnished with tall, wilting plants and a doorman who reminded Beatriz of a waiter in one of those enormous Italian restaurants in the suburbs that her parents refused to go to: stained maroon jacket, black pants, dingy white shirt. He had a military-style hat he was always taking off, to run his hand through slick black hair flecked with dandruff. He never spoke to Beatriz when she and her uncle went out for an occasional walk or to rent a video, but he always said hello to her uncle in an obsequious way.

The upper floors of the building were all the same: long, dim halls, door after door fitted with brass numbers set above glass knobs, fan-shaped sconces lighting cream-colored walls. She rarely saw any of the other tenants, and most of the ones she did see were elderly. On the few occasions when she heard young, lively voices in the hall and she ran to the peephole to look, there was never anyone there.

It was an eerie place in general, but the oddest thing of all—until the face appeared in the wood, that is—was the carpeting in the halls. It, too, was cream-colored, with a pale green ivy pattern along the edges.

Little green katydids with piercing black eyes stared up at her, partly hidden in the foliage, sometimes looking as if they were moving in that jittery way crickets and related species have. At first Beatriz thought it was a trick of the light—often they didn't seem to move at all, and at other times they appeared quite agitated. Unlike the face in the wood, they were always perfectly still when she stared at them directly, even if she had just seen them wiggling out of the corner of her eye. She pointed this out to her uncle and asked if he had ever noticed them. No he hadn't, he said, but what a keen eye you have, my dear.

"Nineteenth floor? Please don't," he said at dinner that night. "Theseus Formica lives up there, and he's a pill. He hates children—throws sticks at them in the park and then pretends he didn't do it. He's complained about you several times, though you're quiet as a mouse."

Well. Now that it was off-limits, she was determined to go, the next time her uncle went out.

She awoke the following morning with a sense of anticipation. She finally had something to do besides sit and worry. After the usual strained conversation at breakfast ("Cereal, please," . . . "Thanks . . ."), she dressed for exploration: brown corduroy pants, plain white button-down-collar shirt, hair in a ponytail tucked through the back of a Yankees baseball cap. She pretended to read until her uncle, sighing, went out. She went to the window and watched him cross the street,

made sure the hall was clear (which it always was anyway), and then, heart pounding, pushed the UP button
for the elevator.

She felt self-conscious taking the elevator. In the
otherwise tomblike atmosphere of the apartment building, it was embarrassingly loud. And it looked funny: It
had a door like the door to a regular room, one that you
pulled open on hinges.

It rattled up to their floor, and the brass grating
inside the door clattered back. With a nervous look
behind her, she went in and pressed the top button, the
one for the nineteenth floor. The light behind the button didn't come on, but the grating clanked shut, and
she felt the momentary heaviness as the machinery
started up. Sixteen. Seventeen. Eighteen. The elevator
slowed and jerked to a stop at nineteen.

The grating slid back in complete silence. Standing
on tiptoe, she tried to peer through the window of the
outer door. Too high. She cautiously pushed the door
open.

The hall was not quite the same as the others.
There were the familiar wooden doors with their glass
knobs and brass numerals, the light fixtures, and the
ivy pattern in the carpeting. But the walls were wall-
papered, in a pattern of alternating stripes about an
inch wide. Half the stripes were cream-colored, and
half were dark red, just a little redder than the brown
wood of the doors. It gave this hall a different feeling:
older, richer, more official.

No sign of nasty old whatshisname. She jumped as the elevator grating closed and the cage began its noisy descent—someone must have pressed the call button on a lower floor. A tiny insect face stared up at her from the carpet, still except for its mouth parts, which worked as if it was chewing something. She shuddered. Here the insects were moving even when she looked right at them.

"And no sign of Home Furnishings." Her voice sounded awfully loud.

She couldn't see anything to the left or right except doors and wall fixtures, the pale carpet, and the striped walls disappearing in the distance. She imagined it as a funeral home, behind each door a casket on display in subdued light, with large flower arrangements and quietly weeping relatives. *Ugh. Don't think about that.*

After hesitating briefly over the decision about which way to turn, she went left—because she had to go in one direction or the other, and that was just what she decided.

Once or twice she thought she heard people talking in low voices behind the doors she passed, but when she stood still to listen, there was only silence. Before long she realized she had walked farther than she could have on her uncle's floor without coming to the end of the hallway. *It must be bigger on the upper floors,* she thought, not considering how unusual that would be.

The katydids in the carpeting were moving quite

vigorously now. She could see them hopping away as she passed, looking almost like popcorn popping.

And here was another odd thing: The stripes in the wallpaper seemed to be waving about ever so slightly, as though they were rustling in a breeze. But, like the katydids downstairs, when she looked hard at them, they were still. Something was wrong with the doors, too. They weren't straight, they were warped, door and frame together—as they might appear through old-fashioned, rippled window glass.

The dim light from the wall lamps cast grotesque shadows—as if spiders, trapped in the shades, had died, their bodies and legs throwing branchy patterns on the floor and ceiling. Bending down, she touched a real ivy leaf stuck into the carpeting.

She straightened up and went on, trying to make sense of what was happening. The light was now so faint, she couldn't see clearly. Was that a pattern on the ceiling? Was it the stripes on the walls? Thin, twisting shapes rose from either side to meet overhead, like branches over a path in a forest. *Well, that's what it looks like, anyway*, she thought. *Like I'm on a nature hike.* She stopped for a moment. *But it wouldn't be this dark at ten in the morning.*

She could no longer tell the doors from the wallpaper. She couldn't see the knobs and numbers, and the wood split from the bottom up into thick, ribbon-like shapes—like the curvy wallpaper stripes. It was as if she was walking through a forest of thin, wavy trees growing out of the floor. She shook her head, and just as she began to think she'd better turn back, she realized that those *were* trees growing up out of the floor. The lamps had become points of light, small and far away; stars winking as they were more or less obscured by the dark red and brown saplings lining the path of the young forest in which she was walking.

She looked back. A few yards behind her the hall shimmered. Ahead was a darkening forest. She took a deep breath and kept going.

3

A BRUSH WITH DEATH

THE PATH WOUND THROUGH BIRCH AND MADRONE, live oak and bay trees. Moss and ferns covered the forest floor—what she could see of it, since the daylight was fading. Birds twittered softly, putting one another to bed, and an occasional soft crunch in the underbrush signaled a small animal making its way out into the night.

She had always liked walking alone in the woods in Iowa, and although she had no idea how she'd come to be here—wherever *here* was—in some ways she felt more at home in this forest than she did in New York's Central Park, where there were always so many people. She was as social as the next person, but there was something basic and comforting about being away from everybody, about being by yourself in the woods. Your problems were somewhere else, and here it was just you and the birds and the trees and the ferns. Unless, of course, you got stung by a bee.

In the fading light, she had to concentrate on following the path to avoid the roots and stones poking up out of the hard brown dirt, so she didn't notice right away that someone or something was walking behind her. And when she did, she tried to convince herself it was just the echo of her own footsteps—until she heard a twig crack.

She turned to face the sound, ready to yell at whatever it was—or run.

You have no doubt seen pictures of the famous

black figure of Death. He carries a scythe, his face is hidden by a hood, and he's a skeleton beneath his robes. Imagine how you'd feel if you actually met him, walking alone in a strange forest at nightfall. Beatriz was too terrified to move—and too terrified to speak.

"Why, hello there." The voice was friendly. Not what she expected. "Please don't be alarmed at my appearance. It's a costume. I've learned that people expect a certain dramatic touch." He sighed. "But yes, I am Death. The Grim Reaper. Your Eternal Reward. Whatever." There was a rotting smell in the air, like bad breath or very strong cheese. It made Beatriz feel faint.

"Have I . . . that is . . ."

"No, no! Goodness, no! You haven't 'passed on.' It's not yet 'your time.' This is a purely casual encounter."

"But where am I?" she asked.

"Hmm. You know, I really couldn't say. We're just coming out of a forest here and into some hills. . . . I used to be a real whiz at places, but I've forgotten so much since I got this satellite positioning gizmo. When it's working correctly, it's supposed to tell you your exact latitude and longitude, right down to the meter." He held up a device that looked like a cell phone, clicked it, then brought it up under his hood for a closer look. "But these cheap batteries . . ."

An unsettling thought came to Beatriz. "We *are* still on Earth, though, right?"

"Oh, yes." He looked around hesitantly. "At least, I *think* so."

It was now almost dark, and the robed figure took a flashlight out of his sleeve and shone it ahead of them, indicating that they should keep walking. They went on side by side, Beatriz wondering what he would do if she tried to excuse herself so she could find the hallway and go back to Uncle M's. But after a few nervous glances at the black robe and the silvery blade of the scythe, she decided to keep quiet for the time being.

The birds had settled down, but chirping insects, joined by dozens of peeping frogs, made the warm night air feel happy and friendly. A moon (it *looked* like Earth's moon) peered over the edge of the forest and soon rose high enough to make the flashlight unnecessary. Thousands of stars twinkled above them in a big black sky. Beatriz tried to make out the Big Dipper, or Orion, but there were so many stars, and the ones she was looking for either were not there or were lost in the bright ocean of light that spread across the sky.

Now the path took them through low, grassy hills dotted with live oaks and their velvety brown shadows. Behind them, the forest was a thick, dark blanket.

"Well," said her companion meaningfully, "I have a confession to make."

Beatriz stopped, somewhat alarmed.

"Nothing to get worked up about. I exaggerated a little bit in saying this was a casual encounter. True, it's unofficial, but I did ask that wood imp in your uncle's apartment to mention that the top floor might be worth exploring."

"Is this about my parents?" Although frightened, Beatriz was hopeful that he might know something about their disappearance.

"Well . . . yes and no." He paused.

"What do you mean?" She wished she could see his face underneath that hood. Or maybe not.

"Let me give you a little background—how things function in my line of work. First of all, it's very bureaucratic. It wasn't that way 'in the Beginning,' when they set things up, but rules have a way of breeding more rules—they're worse than rabbits. For every person I take in, there are a dozen forms to fill out. Names to be entered in registries, notifications of final destination made—the regulations book is as thick as a Bible.

"So when someone throws a wrench into the works, there's a lot of explaining to do. A lot of extra paperwork for yours truly."

"What do you mean, 'throws a wrench'? Did my parents . . ."

He ignored her question and began walking again. "Unfortunately, there are also very strict confidentiality rules."

She stood looking at him for a moment, then ran to catch up.

"I can't tell you much," he continued. "The Big Guy doesn't like the general public to know about the inner workings. Shrouds things in mystery. Claims it keeps people on their toes."

"But what about my mom and dad? What did you mean by it's 'yes and no' about them? You *have* to tell me if they're—if they're . . ."

"Well, the 'no' part means I can't really tell you much."

"And the 'yes'?"

"The 'yes'?" He sounded pained. "The 'yes' . . ." His voice trailed off.

"Are they alive?" She touched his sleeve but immediately pulled her hand back. His robe was freezing cold, quite a shock on a warm summer's evening. "Are they *here?*"

"Lovely night, isn't it?" said her companion. Then, after a pause, "Let me just say I know that your parents—and you, for that matter—are not the sort of people who go around throwing wrenches into things. But there are others who do. And if I don't want to spend the better part of Eternity filling out wrongful death certificates and illegal otherworldly transfer filings, some of those others—one very clever one, in particular, who has managed to turn the regulations to her advantage—need to be dealt with. I could nab her in a minute," he glanced at his scythe, "if she weren't such a slippery character. She's made it bloody complicated, pardon the expression. Your typical death row appeal is like a stroll in the park in comparison."

"I see." Beatriz didn't.

"So—I'm asking for a little unofficial help."

"From me?"

"Yes," he said.

"It *is* about my parents—right?"

"Just look at that lovely moon."

Beatriz let her frustration get the better of her fear. "How can I help if you won't tell me what's going on? What am I supposed to do? Where am I supposed to go?"

"First off, you can't hang around *me* much longer. You'll start to grow moss on your face, and your toes'll turn gray. (You don't want to know what happens after that.) You're going to have to figure a lot of it out on your own, because I *cannot* be perceived as being involved. I'm bending the rules just by talking to you."

"Rules? What rules?"

"I'll try to keep an eye on you, though my schedule's awfully hectic, what with the Middle East and all. But if you can manage to help me, you may possibly help yourself, too. No guarantees. Not even I know . . ."

"What?"

"Hush. I've said too much." As he said this, a faint flash of sheet lightning lit the sky behind the distant hills, and a low roll of thunder followed a few seconds later. "He's omnipresent. When He's paying attention."

They walked on in silence.

"Look, there's light up there, just around the bend," said Death. "Let's see if we can't get you a room for the night."

The path curved around the base of one last hill, and Beatriz paused for a moment on the other side to admire a dramatically changed view. Below them, a quarter mile or so down a gentle grassy slope dotted with fireflies, a great river spread out across the landscape, black except where a bright blade of moonlight fell across it. And just ahead, the path joined a one-lane dirt road that wound its way down to a little village at the water's edge. The lights of a city twinkled on the far side of the river near the horizon.

"How beautiful!" Beatriz said. A gentle breeze cooled her face as she watched water flow through the slice of moonlight.

"Yes . . . lovely," said Death. "And so fraught with metaphor."

Following the road, which eventually turned into a paved street, they soon found themselves flanked by darkened houses, widely spaced, with neatly trimmed lawns and hedges between. They passed a hardware store and a bank, and stopped in front of a small hotel: brown-shingled, two stories high, with four windows across the front on each floor. A white sign hung over a door in the middle of the ground floor. THE LIBRARY—RESTAURANT & LODGINGS was painted in elegant black script. There was just one light on, in a window next to the door, and the place seemed deserted.

She turned to the robed figure to say, "It doesn't look like anyone's still up," but he was gone. A nasty smell lingered in the air.

She wrinkled her nose and knocked softly. Holding her breath, she could hear nothing but the steady drip of water from a garden faucet nearby. She knocked again.

The porch light came on, and after a few seconds the door swung inward. A distinguished-looking older man with a large nose, thinning gray hair, and beautiful white eyebrows asked, "Who's there?" He stared over her shoulder, and she realized he was blind.

"I wonder if I could use your phone. I need to call my uncle."

The man smiled mysteriously and said, "You must be quite lost, my dear, to be wandering around here at this time of night. But come in, come in. The night air is rank with the smell of death."

"Yes . . . I know."

4
THE LIBRARY

BEATRIZ FOUND HERSELF in a cozy room outfitted as a hotel lobby. An electric fan on the reception desk quietly pushed the warm air around. Three sofas the size of rowboats crowded in on an empty stone fireplace, competing for space with a side table and floor lamp. A staircase with an ornate wooden banister rose into darkness. The muffled ticking of a clock upstairs was the only sound aside from the soft whirring of the fan.

"I am Borges," said the man, "and this is my inn. You may try the telephone there on the desk, but getting a connection is difficult. And sometimes there is an echo. Often there is . . . an echo." He paused, seemingly lost in thought, then said, "Dial nine first."

"Thank you very much. My name is Beatriz." She dialed Uncle M's number. It rang faintly, but there was no answer.

That's funny, she thought. His voice mail should have picked up. She set the receiver down and wondered what she should do next.

The old man was reaching out to touch his fingertips to the surface of a mirror on the wall next to the desk. With frightening precision, his sightless eyes stared directly into hers in the glass, and she thought for a moment that he could see. But his gaze drifted away, and he said, "Have they cleaned this? Are there spots?"

"It looks fine to me," she said. "No one answered."

There was an awkward silence.

"Well, we had better find you a room," said Borges, sighing. "It's almost eleven, and you are far from home."

"How do you know? How do you know I'm far from home?"

"Everyone who comes here is far from home. We're quite the outpost."

"Is that New York across the river?"

"New York? No, certainly not New York. I'm sorry. But let's talk tomorrow. It's late, and I must close up for the night. Let me get you settled in." He felt for the rack of keys and unhooked one. "Fortunately, we have a number of unoccupied rooms." He gave a little laugh.

"I'll put you in number 26. It is already made up. Forgive me if I don't show you up. . . . It's getting hard for me to take the stairs." He clicked a wall switch, and warm yellow light cascaded down from the upper floor. "There are sandwiches and milk by the bed. The bath is at the end of the hall. We'll try the telephone again in the morning."

Beatriz stuck out her tongue at him as he spoke, but he didn't react. He really was blind. She watched him turn and shuffle off toward the back, down two steps into a darkened lounge. She thought he was going to bump into another mirror at the far end, but he turned aside just in time. With the click of a door latch, she was alone.

It was a relief leaving the gloom of the lobby, coming up into the bright, soft light upstairs. She had never before stayed by herself in a hotel, though her uncle's apartment building felt like one, and she had often been very much alone there. This place seemed more like someone's home.

Still, she felt rather grown up, holding the key and looking for her room.

She found herself in a hall with dark blue carpeting *(No katydids, thank goodness)*, six or seven rooms going off on either side, and a grandfather clock ticking quietly near the end.

None of the rooms had numbers.

I can't try them all—I'll wake everybody up!

The feeling of being grown up dissolved into mild panic.

There must be a system. It's the second floor, so they all start with 2, I suppose. And if the room by the stairs is number 20, let's see . . . the one next to the other end—that must be the bathroom at the end—that would be 27. Unless they start on the other side, or alternate across the hall, in which case . . . In which case, I'm just going to have to try one. She pushed the key as quietly as she could into the lock of one of the doors and attempted to turn it.

It didn't work.

Something bright caught her eye. Mirrors faced each other on both sides of the hall, hung between the doors, and she noticed that the reflection of one of the doors had a big brass numeral 23 right in the middle of it. *Well, that's a help,* she thought, turning to the door. But there was no number. She touched the wood. It was smooth, dark, and bare. She looked in the mirror again. There was the number—backward of course, but right in the middle of the door.

Looking in the mirror on the opposite wall, she discovered that the door facing number 23 was marked 26.

Okay. At least there was a system, though not of the usual sort. Now the key turned, and the door swung quietly inward. She felt along the wall inside and found the light switch.

The room was small, painted white, with a pleasantly old-fashioned quilt-covered bed, two side tables, and a flip-front desk—the kind her uncle called a secretary. There was a door that looked as though it ought to lead to a closet, and a window hidden behind pale blue curtains.

The side table closest to her had on it a plate with two sandwiches, a small pitcher of milk, and an empty glass. She sat on the bed and looked at the sandwiches. Cucumber and mayonnaise on white toast. Still warm! She bit into one, a little nervously at first, then wolfed the whole thing down. *Usually,* she thought, *you end up writhing around on the floor and dying ten minutes later. In stories, anyway.*

But nothing happened, so she ate the other sandwich and then examined the room. Dust bunnies under the bed. Coat hangers and extra blankets in the closet. In the secretary was a large volume from an encyclopedia. ANDREA DORIA through ANTLER. *There must be an*

awful lot of books in that set. There was also a pen, and sta-
tionery printed at the top with a picture of an open
book and the words "The Library, Crescent City."

Then her heart nearly stopped. For there, just
below the rack of pigeonholes in the secretary, lay a
framed black-and-white photograph of her mother and
father posed next to each other in front of the entrance
to Borges's inn. They were smiling, but they looked
rigid and uncomfortable. It had to have been taken several years ago, since they looked quite a bit younger
than now.

She picked it up and stared at it. Tears trickled down
her cheeks, dropping onto the glass.

"How can they . . . ? Where . . . ?"

A familiar feeling returned to her chest: an aching
pain, the physical need to be with them. She sobbed
and looked up at the ceiling. All the feelings that she
had put on hold during her adventure flooded back.
How did this picture get here? Where were they?

Nearly blinded by tears, she stumbled to the door
and down the stairs, clutching the picture, tripping on
the steps leading to the lounge. Trying to compose herself, she knocked on the door the old man had gone
through.

No answer. She tried to keep her mouth from
grimacing, tried to keep her tears in check.

She knocked again. "Excuse me!"

Still no answer.

She turned the knob. The door led to a darkened

restaurant dining room. Glowing white tablecloths seemed to float above the floor in the moonlight. The wall on the right was all windows, overlooking the glittering river. At the far end of the room, the hotel proprietor sat at one of the window tables, his back to her. He might have been asleep or lost in thought, except that he was drumming his fingers on the table and humming softly.

"Excuse me, sir." She went over to him. "I was in the room and I found this picture. . . . It's my mother and father and they're missing and that was why I came to stay with my uncle—until we find them—and I need to know where they are, where you got this. Please." She couldn't hold back her tears anymore.

He said nothing. He didn't seem to have heard her.

"Please. PLEASE!" She swiped at the tears.

The old man turned toward her. "Photograph?" He cleared his throat. "Photograph? They are so . . . so unreal." He shook his head. "In the end, they're just paper. Just pieces of paper."

"Can you *please* help me?"

"Yes, yes, of course. I will try. Let me see if we can find something." He stood up wearily and, with a gesture indicating that she should follow him, walked to the back of the dining room and through swinging silver doors into the kitchen. Rows of hanging stainless steel pots gleamed faintly in the darkness. A computer screen glowed green next to a small desk.

"Please sit down. And type in, oh, I suppose, 'photograph in the rooms.' That would be a good place to start."

Beatriz tapped out the words and pressed ENTER. The display went blank for a moment, and then a long list began slowly scrolling down the screen. As far as she could tell, it was largely composed of random words and phrases. There were occasional coherent entries: "Egyptian Tombs in Cross Section" and "Collisions at Sea, 1700–1750," for example, and "Jim's Fortieth Birthday," "Cheeses of Bavaria," and "Health Cults in 19th-Century Saratoga." Before she had time to wonder whether her mother and father had ever been to Bavaria, "Recent Guests at The Library, Crescent City" appeared.

She tracked it with the cursor and clicked on it.

Three photographs came up on the screen: an empty room that looked like the one she was staying in; a very thick hardcover book half submerged in murky water; and the interior of another room, similar to the first. The computer flashed a message at the bottom of the screen: "Click HERE for more detail."

"Did you find something? It's in such disarray. . . . I'm not well suited as a librarian anymore." He pointed to his eyes.

"I'm not sure. It looks like the room upstairs. And a book."

She clicked on HERE.

The machine prompted: "Enter last name, first name, middle initial."

"It's asking me to enter a name. What should I do?"

"Type in your name, I suppose."

Immediately after she did this, the screen filled completely with text—an enormous number of words scrolling slowly down what seemed an infinitely long page. This time nearly everything was recognizable. It was a jumble of personal facts, quotes, letters, anecdotes: her grandma's note to her on her tenth birthday, grocery lists, poems, transcriptions of telephone calls. There was frequent mention of herself, her mother, and her father.

She wanted to stop everything and rewind it, to go back to that life, to the world she had so taken for granted before the events of the past two weeks. Or at least keep the words on the page from disappearing. She clicked all over the screen, but the words continued moving up and out of view. "How do I stop it?"

"Stop it? Stop it? You can't stop it, my dear. It's Time. It's the past, falling away . . . falling into darkness."

She glared at him. What was he talking about? Why he did have a picture of her parents? Why did his computer have so much personal information about her family?

She looked back at the screen, which was now blank except for a blinking cursor and the words "Click HERE for next entry."

The next entry turned out to be a picture of an unfamiliar housecat grooming itself.

She was too exhausted and too miserable to hide

her anger. "What is going on here? Who put that picture in my room?"

"Now, now. Please calm down. It could have been
anyone. . . . So many pass through here. Let's think about
it in the morning, when you can look at it in the light.
Perhaps there's writing on the back? We'll see, we'll see.
I really must be getting to bed."

She held the photo up in the dim light but could
see nothing.

Back in her room, she slid the picture out of its
frame to see if there was anything written on the back.
Nothing. And on the front, just the image, the flesh
tones faintly hand-tinted—something she hadn't
noticed before. She slipped it back into the frame.

What was that book doing, the one in the picture
on the computer? Floating? *Books don't float—do they?*
And what about the photographs of the two rooms?

She stared at the forced smiles frozen on her parents' faces. Her eyes ached and her head hurt. She lay
back on the bed, holding the picture close to her chest.
There were no more tears left, but she sobbed silently
until she finally fell asleep.

5

THE DOCKS

BEATRIZ WOKE THE NEXT MORNING to the sound of clattering silverware on plates outside her room. A delicious smell of bacon and coffee seeped in under the door. She stood up stiffly, having slept in her clothes, and, still holding the picture, looked out into the hall. There was a tray on the floor with a covered dish, a half grapefruit in a bowl, a carafe of coffee, and a cup.

"Ugh!" she said, tasting the coffee. "Why do they *drink* this stuff?" But the grapefruit was sweet, and there were scrambled eggs and toast, five pieces of bacon, and lots of strawberry jam.

She felt better. She'd found a clue—though she had no idea what to make of it. After eating, she washed her face with a cold, wet washcloth, smoothed out her clothes as best she could, and took the photograph downstairs.

She expected a busy scene—perhaps someone asking at the front desk for a morning paper, guests hurrying in to breakfast or hovering around their luggage, checking out. But there was no one in the reception area. The only sounds were the ticking of the upstairs-hall clock and the whirring of the fan on the desk. She went into the dining room, where the sun blazed through the windows and reflections from the water danced on the ceiling. The old man sat in the same spot as the night before, playing a game of chess by himself.

"Good morning, dear child. I'm sorry about last

night. I have to get someone in here to look at that computer. It hasn't been the same since the spaghetti sauce incident."

"I have the picture," Beatriz said. "I've got it right here."

"You know, I have an idea. Why don't you show it to my friend Rose? She's very good at mysteries. She may even have put it there herself—she's been a great help to me, decorating. And frankly," he added, tapping his temple to emphasize his sightless eyes, "it won't do much good for me to look at it."

"Oh, yes. I'm sorry. May I try calling my uncle again?"

The old man sighed. "The telephone's out. Something must have happened to the cable. Did you enjoy your breakfast?"

"Yes. Thank you. It was very nice." She hesitated. "Can you tell me where I can find your friend?"

"Of course. Simply go out the front door and turn left, then walk along the river to the wharf area. There are only a few commercial buildings. One of them is a warehouse: concrete, just one story but quite tall, with five windows. On the side facing the river is the office, adjacent to the docks. Rose will be the only one there. It's the off-season, you know."

Beatriz wondered whether *every* season here was the off-season, but she thanked him politely and said she would have her uncle send money to pay for the room when she got in touch with him.

"Oh, no, my dear, please. Consider it a gift. Sleep is truly a gift, you know. A gift denied so many . . ."

She left him to his chess.

The town looked amazingly different in daylight. Beatriz was surprised at how small and empty it was, and how immense the river seemed. She saw just a few other people: two men sitting on the shady porch of a white clapboard cottage, leaning back in their chairs, watching a baby play in the grass between the house and the dusty street; a girl lazily hanging laundry out to dry; a young man washing the wheelhouse windows of the two-car ferry tied up at a dock.

A breeze blew off the water, giving the town an open feeling that made it seem even more deserted. A line of trees was just visible on the far side of the river, and beyond that the buildings of a small city. On this side, a dense forest began just upriver from where she was, and downstream the channel disappeared into the low hills she had walked through the night before.

The warehouse wasn't hard to find. It was at the water's edge, near a pier that ran a dozen or so yards out into the river. A pleasant lapping sound echoed through the pilings.

There wasn't any sign, but Beatriz found the office door and went in. If ever it had been a busy, working office, it wasn't now. Two steel desks were piled with carelessly stacked papers and manila folders. An old black telephone acted as a paperweight for one stack, and there was a typewriter on the floor, serving as a doorstop. A filing cabinet stood against one bare wall, a single wilting white tulip in a mayonnaise jar overhanging the front of it.

Sitting in a chair at one of the desks was one of the oddest-looking people Beatriz had ever seen.

She was a middle-aged woman, heavyset, with long, carelessly brushed strawberry blond hair, dressed in white overalls that shone faintly all the colors of the rainbow, like an opal. From her back, through hemmed slits in a blue work shirt, sprouted a set of four wings, each about two feet long. They looked like rumpled dragonfly wings, neatly flanking the crossed shoulder straps of the overalls.

This couldn't be the "she" that Death was talking about, could it? The one who was throwing a wrench into the works? She certainly didn't look very dangerous.

The woman was concentrating hard on writing something—her tongue stuck out one side of her mouth, and she didn't appear to notice Beatriz.

"Dang! They just won't go the right way! Why does that *m* look like an *n*? Let's see . . . 'muffler,' 'muffler,' hmm. How many *f*'s are *in* that word?"

"Excuse me," Beatriz spoke timidly. "Excuse me. The man at the hotel—Mr. Borges—said I should ask for Rose. It's about a picture in one of the rooms."

The woman looked up with a start. Her face was red with irritation. "Can you spell?" she demanded.

"Sometimes."

"Well, how do you spell 'muffler'? I can't for the life of me get all these letters going the same direction."

Beatriz folded her hands and looked up at a nail in the wall. "Let's see. . . . 'Muffler.' M–U–F–F–L–E–R. 'Muffler.'"

"Thanks, honey." The woman wrote it out, peered at it suspiciously, set the paper down, and stabbed a period triumphantly at the bottom. "So . . . what's this about the hotel?"

"Mr. Borges told me to ask for Rose. He said she might have put this picture in my room."

"Oh, he said that, did he?" As she spoke, she took a spray can from the desk, then craned her neck around and sprayed a sweet-smelling mist on her wings, which perked up and began to look a little more dashing. "Glad to make your acquaintance. I'm Rose."

"I—I'm Beatriz. Are those . . . real?" Beatriz asked.

"Excuse me? Isn't that a bit of a personal question? People ever ask you if you're wearing a wig?"

"I'm sorry, it's just that I've never met anyone with wings before."

"Yeah, well, they're real, all right. And a real nuisance, too, for all their la-di-da 'Hi, I'm your fairy-dang-godmother.' Not worth the trouble anymore. When I was your age, I'd be flitting around from here to there— 'flower to flower,' as we used to say—meaning boy to boy. They're for youngsters. I can't even get up off the ground anymore. Useless. And a royal pain to take care of." The wings gleamed, smooth and fresh, and for all her sour talk, Rose seemed to be fanning them rather proudly. "So, let's see this picture. I'm not surprised Borges can't figure out the stuff he's got—he can't keep track of his own fingernails."

Beatriz held out the picture to Rose, who put on a pair of bright red reading glasses to study it. "It's my parents. I found it at the hotel, and I don't know how it got there. They're—they're gone, and I have to find them."

"Nice-lookin' couple. And they're 'gone'?"

"Yes," said Beatriz. "I came home from school, and . . ." She had to work to keep her voice steady. ". . . and they weren't there. Have you seen them? That looks like Mr. Borges's inn behind them."

"Yes, it does. And yes, I did see 'em, or folks looking something like 'em."

Beatriz felt a surge of hope mixed with fear. Somewhat overwhelmed, she collapsed with as much grace as she could muster onto a chair next to the desk. Rose looked at her coolly for a moment, then went on. "It was kind of from a distance, and these eyes aren't what they used to be. Couple of weeks ago. Had their granny or somebody along for the ride. Charon—he's the ferryman and local go-to guy for ship work—took all three of 'em upriver." She put her glasses down.

"Do you know where they went?" Beatriz asked. *And who is this granny?*

"Riverrun." Rose smiled. "He took 'em up to Riverrun."

6
A SENSE OF DIRECTION

"THE NAME RIVERRUN is from a book by an old friend of mine," said Rose. "Didn't make a heck of a lot of sense overall, but he sure could turn a phrase. Jim—that's his name—he retired from the literary business some time ago and runs a busted-up old resort now: Riverrun. About forty miles upstream."

"Can we call to see if they're still there?"

"No phone service up that way."

"Oh. Well, how do you get there? Is there a bus?"

"A bus? A *bus?* Where'd you say you were from? There's no bus out here. There isn't even a road—just a hunter's trail." Rose put her glasses on again and consulted a chart taped to her desk.

"Where's the man who took them up the river? I'll ask him. My uncle can send the money."

"Charon? He's strictly on a cash-only basis. I oughta know."

"Well, then I'll *walk!*" Beatriz was shaking slightly, angry at the woman's condescending tone. "Which way is it?"

"Calm down, kid. No need to get all worked up. But you can't walk there—it's forty miles! And there aren't any hotels like Mr. Borges's on the way, either." Rose surveyed Beatriz over the top of her glasses again. "Listen," she said, more gently. "I hate to see a young person all distressed and everything. Let's show your picture to Charon. If he recognizes 'em, I'll run you up there myself. Take a coupla days on the barge. River depth's good, and it's kind of a slow week. I need a break from these papers anyway. God-awful tax audit is what it is."

Beatriz, as desperate people sometimes do when help arrives, instantly stopped being angry and became overly grateful. "Would you really? Oh, thank you! Thank you so much!"

"Simmer down, simmer down. Don't get all worked up just yet. Let's see what Charon has to say."

They walked down the wharf to the boat landing, and the ferryman said that yes, those were two of the people he had taken up to Riverrun. ("Though it isn't a very flattering shot, is it?")

Beatriz felt almost lightheaded as they walked back to the warehouse. They were going up the river, and there she'd find her mom and dad. Simple as that. She almost felt silly for having been so emotional over the whole situation.

"Now," said Rose, gathering together all the papers on her desk and stuffing them into the top drawer, "let me just round up those two brats of mine and get the barge ready. You go back for your bags and tell Borges where we're going. What? No bags? How the heck do you expect to get on without any clothes? Never mind. I have some things might fit you. May be a tad loose, but we'll fix you up."

Rose went to the door and bellowed, "Hey, Thisby!

PYR-a-mus! Get your sorry butts in here this instant! We're going up the river!" She shot a look back at Beatriz and grinned. "Probably off playing with match-es, or breaking and entering. I gave up on 'em some time back."

The sound of shouting children drifted in through the door, then quickly got louder, and a moment later the tired old office exploded in a whirlwind of energy as two children, a boy and a girl, came racing in. They looked to Beatriz to be about eight or nine years old, and both wore green overalls and had a pair of bright blue dragonfly wings sticking out from between the straps on their backs. As they rounded the corner their wings whirred madly, helping them make the turn and slowing them to a stop in front of their mother.

"Kids, I want you to meet someone. Here—what's your name again, honey? Okay—Beatriz. Beatriz . . . what kind of a name is that? Okay now, calm down, you two. This here's Pyramus, who seems unusually clean today—what have you two been up to?—and this is my little ray of sunshine, Thisby." The children grinned in a friendly way at Beatriz, who felt rather awkward in the presence of so many people with wings.

"Are you from across the river?" asked Thisby. "My mom says maybe we can go there next week and get a salamander!"

"No . . . I'm from Des Moines. But I'm staying with my uncle M in New York City." Beatriz was a bit hesi-tant. Did they know where Des Moines was? Or New

York? "We have salamanders in Des Moines. There's one that lives in our basement."

"Oh, Mom, can we go there, please, please, puh-*leeze?*" The children tugged at Rose's sleeve until she shook them off.

"Now, hold on a minute. I don't know what this Des Moines is, and even if I did, why would we go there when we can just take the ferry across the river? I don't know how you talked me into this whole salamander business in the first place. But we'll have to discuss it later. We've got work to do.

"Pyramus, fill up a couple of boxes with provisions from the stockroom—enough for a trip up to Riverrun. Thisby, I want you to go tell Old Man Borges we're going up there, that we'll be gone four or five days, and if he needs anything, he'll have to ask the neighbors."

With a flutter and a yelp, the girl raced out the door and the boy was off into a dark doorway at the back of the office.

"Now, let me just tidy things up a bit here, and we'll be off."

7

ON THE RIVER

THE BARGE was about twice the size of the two-car ferry. It had a black iron hull and deck, which was flat and featureless except for a cabin near the stern just large enough for the wheel, a few coils of rope, and a stairway leading below. An exhaust pipe ran up alongside the wheelhouse, coughing out puffs of smoke to the pleasant *chug-chug* of the engine. The deck had no railing and was empty except for three brightly colored aluminum lawn chairs set up near the bow.

Beatriz stood on deck, looking at her photograph, wondering if the color in her parents' cheeks had been there all along. Had she just been so upset last night that she hadn't noticed it?

The children lugged aboard wooden crates filled with tin cans, boxes of pasta, fruits, vegetables, and two big cartons of milk. Beatriz loved the way they used their wings to keep their balance. She felt a little shy around them, but Thisby, especially, was so friendly that Beatriz could already feel herself warming up to her.

Walking up the gangway, checking the pockets of her overalls, Rose had the satisfied look of a grownup who has finished the hard part of a day and is ready for the fun part.

"Everything shipshape here? Excellent! Clean hull, good weather, no traffic." She squinted out at the river and then looked at Beatriz. "Got your picture? Okey doke—then let's get going." She hauled the gangplank on board as Pyramus, on the dock, cast off the bow line and raced back to cast off the stern. He waited until the boat had almost drifted out of range, then jumped aboard, wings beating furiously.

The engine chugged more loudly as it worked to pull them away from shore. Beatriz sat in one of the lawn chairs and watched the town grow small until it was just a smudge on the horizon, then turned to gaze upriver. A clean breeze ruffled her hair. She could hear laughter and swearing from the wheelhouse. She tilted the picture of her parents to deflect the sun's glare and tried to hold in check the pangs of loneliness. The breeze flapped the edge of her sleeve against the frame. What had they been doing at Borges's inn? She didn't remember ever going there. Was it before she was born? They didn't look *that* much younger. The longer she stared at the picture, the odder her parents' faces seemed: They were posed and smiling, but there was a disturbing, distracted look in their eyes.

After they had been on the water for fifteen or twenty minutes, she went over to the wheelhouse.

"Nice weather, eh?" asked Rose. "We'll make good time." She looked at Beatriz. "You doing okay?"

"Yeah. Just thinking."

"Well, I suppose you got a lot to think about. How long'd you say your folks been gone?"

"Almost three weeks." Beatriz didn't want to talk about their disappearance right now, so she changed the subject. "You . . . your children . . . you have such a nice family."

Rose laughed affectionately. "Nice family, huh? Those two?" She grinned at Beatriz. "Well, they do keep things interesting, that's for sure." She put her hand on Beatriz's shoulder. "Listen, kid, if your folks are anywhere around here, we'll find 'em. Don't you worry. Probably snuck off for a second honeymoon . . . though why they'd go to Riverrun, I don't know."

"Without telling me," added Beatriz sadly. She gazed out the wheelhouse window in silence for a minute before wandering back onto the deck.

The river water was a beautiful pale brown. The sun was high, so when Beatriz looked down, she could see yellow folds of light waving in a halo around the shadow of her head. It reminded her of the halo she saw in the water of the lake where her dad had taken her fishing—the only time they had ever gone fishing—just before the boat capsized.

It was a wide river. Beatriz couldn't see much on the far shore except a thin line of dark green trees. Rose had kept them close to the near shore, about a hundred feet out, so as not to get caught up in the current, which was running against them. There were big, flat upwellings a little farther out, and the water seemed to be racing past—though, watching the land, Beatriz could tell that they weren't moving very fast.

The bank was lined with pine and fir trees right up to the water's edge. Every so often there was a clearing with low bushes, meadow grass, and wildflowers, or a grove of weeping willows. The willow branches overhanging the water created enclosed areas that looked as if they'd be pleasant to row a small boat through. Birds darted among the treetops, and occasionally a log or branch floated by.

She was getting hot, so she went back to the wheelhouse for some shade. Just as she got there, the sound of splintering glass came from below decks. "Geez!" yelled Rose. "Now what? Here, take the wheel—I gotta see what that was. Just keep straight on, and I'll be back in a sec."

Thrown completely off guard, Beatriz gripped the wheel in a state of exhilaration and fear. How could she possibly steer this huge thing? *Okay, stay calm. Just little corrections to keep it straight. Whoa! Too much. Just keep it parallel to the bank. Okay, this isn't so hard. . . . Oops!*

"Thanks, kid." Rose returned and took over. "You're a natural." She cut the engine and went to throw the anchor over the side. "False alarm. Just a milk glass. Almost time for lunch anyway."

Going below together, they found the twins sitting at a table in a cabin with portholes on both sides. An open door in the forward bulkhead led to a hallway with more doors opening off of it. The children were making salami-and-cheese sandwiches.

"Pull up a chair," Rose said. For all her gruff manner, Beatriz thought, she was actually a very nice person.

"Thank you." Beatriz sat down to make herself a sandwich.

"Mom says your parents are gone," said Pyramus.

"Pyramus—" began Rose, but Beatriz broke in. "It's okay. I'm looking for them. Your mom thinks they're at Riverrun."

"Well, I didn't exactly say *that,*" said Rose. "Charon took 'em up there. But that was a couple of weeks ago."

No one spoke. Wavelets lapped pleasantly against the hull.

After a few awkward moments, Thisby looked at Beatriz and said, "Want to see our book of spells?"

Rose exhaled loudly. "Now, really, kids. Remember what happened with that pig? I don't want to have to clean up after anything like *that* again."

"We'll be careful, Mom, we promise!" the twins said in chorus. "Come on, Beatriz!"

Taking a big bite of her sandwich, Beatriz stood up and followed them. They turned off the hallway into one of the cabins, and she ducked her head for the low doorway.

The cabin wall, punctuated by three portholes, sloped in toward the floor. There was a neatly made bed against the inner bulkhead, a dresser with a lamp on top, and a small sofa. Beatriz guessed that this was Rose's cabin.

From the top drawer of the dresser, Thisby removed a thick green book covered with intricate gold designs on the cover and spine. It looked very much like the witchcraft books on her uncle M's forbidden shelf.

And it looked very much like the one Beatriz had seen half covered with water in the picture on Mr. Borges's computer.

The two children sat facing each other on the floor, cross-legged, with the book between them. Beatriz perched nervously on the edge of the sofa. "What kind of spells are in there?" she asked.

"Oh, lots!" said Thisby. "But Mom only lets us do a couple of the easy ones in front. You can't even turn to the pages in the back, the spells are so powerful." She looked at her brother. "What should we do?"

"I don't know. You pick something."

Thisby knit her brows. "Okay. *Not* a pig. How about a python?"

"Right," said Pyramus. "What if it constricts us?"

"Maybe just a baby one? Or how about trying a cat again?"

"Yeah, okay, a cat. But we can't let it out of the circle."

"You draw it."

Pyramus got a piece of chalk from a bowl on top of the dresser, picked a spot on the smooth wood floor, and with one long, careful stroke drew a circle about two feet in diameter.

Thisby looked at it closely. "You have to make sure it's completely closed. It has to overlap."

Beatriz noticed that the book made a very faint buzzing noise, as if it were somehow electrified.

"We found it in the river, just last week," said Pyramus. "Mom says it's a powerful book and she's thinking about selling it online. I think we should keep it."

"You found it in the *river?*" Beatriz asked. This had to be more than coincidence.

"It wasn't even wet!" said Pyramus.

"Want to watch?" Thisby asked.

The children folded their hands in their laps. Not knowing what else to do, Beatriz put her hands together, too. After a few seconds, Thisby opened the book to the title page. Beatriz could see printing on it, but she couldn't tell what it said because all the letters were jiggling and moving around like bugs. Thisby held her hand out flat a few inches above the paper, and the words slowed and finally stopped moving.

She turned to the table of contents. Both children peered at it, and Pyramus said, "'About Cats,' page thirty-five."

Thisby held her hand out over the page again and said, "Thirty-five." When she turned to the next page, "35" was printed in the lower right-hand corner in bright red numerals. There was a lot of text on the page and a small square drawing of a scrawny-looking cat staring out at them.

A blank piece of paper, not bound into the book, lay on the left-hand page. Pyramus picked it up and held it below the right-hand page, level with the bottom. Thisby moved her hand over the printing in a slightly circular motion, and the letters began to jiggle about, moving more and more rapidly. When they were dancing furiously, she tipped the book and brushed the surface of the page down, sweeping all the letters onto the paper Pyramus was holding—where they sat quietly in a small pile. The page in the book was now blank.

"Wow," said Beatriz. She had never particularly believed—or disbelieved—in magic, but it was quite something to see it happening right in front of her.

"Shh," said Thisby.

Setting the book aside on the floor and taking the paper from her brother, she brushed the letters off into the circle. For a moment, Beatriz felt horribly dizzy and had to clutch the arm of the sofa to steady herself.

A small black cat with white paws had materialized in the circle. It was licking its hind leg, but when it noticed the children, it stopped grooming and peered up at them curiously. Beatriz was absolutely astonished. A cat had just appeared out of thin air!

"Hey! This one's alive!" cried Pyramus. "What did you do different?"

"I don't know. But it worked!" Thisby shrieked. "Let's tell Mom!"

The two of them jumped up and, with an excited flurry of wings, went skittering out the door yelling, "Mom! We did a cat, and it's alive! Can we keep it? Please, can we keep it?"

Beatriz looked at the cat, which, after returning her gaze for a moment, went on washing itself. *What else could you do with this book? Could you*—she touched the cover gingerly—*find things? Or people?* A mild charge ran through her fingertips, and the buzzing grew louder. She pulled back her hand.

The children came in looking mournful.

"What's wrong?" asked Beatriz.

"Mom says we have to send it back, for its own good." And indeed the cat looked a little strange now: Beatriz could see the floorboards through the tip of its tail, and the color was draining out of its fur.

"It isn't in pain, is it?" asked Beatriz, who was very fond of animals and wouldn't even kill insects—though she made an exception for mosquitoes.

"Naw," said Pyramus. "Look at it. It's washing itself."

"Mom says it's homework time," said Thisby. "We're studying Distraction."

"Distraction?" asked Beatriz. The two children looked at each other and laughed.

The cat had discovered that something odd was happening to its disappearing tail and was batting at it with a paw. "Hello, kitty. Goodbye, kitty," Thisby said. And then, in a more formal voice, "Eye of newt and skin of toad, pack your paws and hit the road." The confused animal quickly became transparent all over, and with a plaintive mew and a last look up at the children it vanished completely.

"Oh!" said Beatriz. "*That* doesn't look very pleasant for it."

"We can try something else later," said Pyramus. "Mom says you're supposed to come and help with the dishes while we do our homework." And with that, the two children raced out of the room.

Beatriz touched the cover of the book again, feeling the thrill of electricity, and lingered a moment longer. Then she went back to the main cabin, leaving the book on the floor.

8

THE VISITOR

BEATRIZ WAS GLAD Rose was in the wheelhouse and the twins were quiet while she did the dishes. She needed time to think. She didn't want to risk something going wrong if she tried to summon up her parents using the book of spells, or have to send them back, as the children had done with the cat. But maybe it could at least help her find out where they were.

After finishing the dishes, she went up to the wheelhouse to talk to Rose about it. But Rose cut her off just as she began, insisting that it was important she know how to weigh and drop anchor, where to find the fire extinguishers, and how to read the river depth from the sonar. ("Trickiest part of the river is coming up tomorrow—might need you to help out on short notice.") After that she asked Beatriz to go below and scrub the stovetop in the galley. It was perfectly clean, but Beatriz dutifully scrubbed it anyway.

Around five o'clock they dropped anchor and made shepherd's pie and salad for dinner. Of course, there were more dishes to wash after that. It seemed clear to Beatriz that Rose was giving her things to do so she wouldn't have a quiet moment to ask about the book.

After dinner they all went up on deck to lie on a thick blanket and look up at the stars. The barge rocked gently, and a warm breeze smelled alternately of muddy water and pine trees. Rose sang in a high, soft, and

51

unexpectedly beautiful voice, songs Beatriz didn't know, songs about love and horses, songs that made her homesick. (There was also one about a sailor and his several girlfriends that she thought wasn't really appropriate for younger children.) She dozed on and off, listening to the songs and the sounds of the water quietly sloshing around the sides of the barge. The twins counted bats skittering above the greeny black silhouette of the forest, darker even than the blue black of the sky.

Rose led a sleepy Beatriz to a cabin with bunk beds and a sink, and gave her an oversized T-shirt in place of pajamas. She said good night and was on her way out the door when Beatriz asked, "Is there anything in that book that might help me find my mom and dad?"

Rose stopped and sighed, her back to Beatriz. "I knew you were going to ask me that sooner or later." She turned and sat down on the edge of the bed. "To be honest, I don't know. There's a whole lot of powerful stuff in there, and a lot of it's stuff nobody ought to mess with, especially amateurs."

She shook her head. "I'm no good at magic. If I'd paid more attention in school and not been so danged interested in the opposite sex, I might've been better at it, but one thing I do have is the good sense not to mess with things I don't understand. A cat's one thing, but we don't want to take a chance on something happening to your folks if we screw up, even if we're just looking for 'em. Better stay away from it. Your mom and dad are probably lounging around Riverrun, sippin' lemonade and having a little vacation. We'll be there soon enough."

"You wouldn't go on a trip without telling your kids, would you?" Beatriz asked.

"Well, you know, sometimes I've been tempted. But, no, I guess I wouldn't."

Beatriz was silent for a moment, then said, "I saw a picture of it. Your book. Floating in the water. On Mr. Borges's computer, when I searched it for stuff about the photograph."

"That's good. Let's talk about it in the morning, okay? You get yourself some shuteye now. It's getting late." Rose patted the quilt and left.

Beatriz was disappointed. She slid out of her under-wear, got up for a minute to rinse it out in the sink, and hung it up to dry. Snuggling back under the covers, she resolved to take a private look at the book. Not try anything, of course, just look.

The next thing she knew, it was morning, and Thisby was standing by her bed, tugging at the quilt and gig-gling. Her wings were fluttering in excitement.

"Get up! There's a whale or something swimming alongside us. Mom says it's awful far inland for a whale, but it's as big as a house!"

"What?" asked Beatriz sleepily.

"A whale! It's right next to us, on the other side. You can see it from the deck. Come on!" She watched

impatiently as Beatriz sat up and pulled on her underwear and dirty corduroys. "Mom said to give you this."
Beatriz took the faded blue work shirt, which had slits
in the back for wings, and put it on over her T-shirt.
"And she said we're going to do a good wash today and
clean you up."

"A whale? Is it following us?" Beatriz zipped up her
pants.

"Pyramus thinks it's following *you!*"

"Why would a whale be following me?"

"Because you're from a different world. Maybe it's a
guardian angel from your world."

"What do you mean I'm from a different world?"

"You said so. New York, right?"

"New York isn't a world, silly, it's a city." Beatriz
wondered why, if they weren't on Earth, everybody
here spoke English.

"Come *on,* it's probably gone by now!" Thisby ran
ahead, racing up the stairs as Beatriz hurried barefoot
after her.

The sunlight on the water was dazzling, but
Beatriz could see the great dark form keeping pace
with them, about five yards out and a few feet under.
It was roughly whalelike in shape, sleek and brownish
black, and about a third the length of the barge.
Pyramus was leaning dangerously over the side, stabil-
ized by furiously whirring wings, talking nonstop to
himself about how they might be able to snare it with
the anchor chain.

Rose was in the wheelhouse. "Friend of yours?" She nodded toward the beast. "Been pacing us ever since I got up four hours ago. Big as a dinosaur."

"What is it?" Beatriz asked.

"For all I know, it *is* a dinosaur." Rose's wings fluttered anxiously.

"Could it be a whale? I mean, one that got lost and wandered up here by mistake?"

"Well, that's my guess. We're only twenty miles from the ocean. Maybe it thinks we're a whale, too. It's not doing anything but swimming next to us, so it doesn't seem to be too much of a threat at the moment. But I want the three of you to take turns watching it. I don't like surprises, especially big ones, and I've got to pay attention to the navigation."

Beatriz went back to the edge of the deck and told the twins what their mother had said. Pyramus was now speculating aloud about how he might lasso it with a rope and ride on its back and didn't seem to hear her, but Thisby immediately sat down cross-legged, shaded her eyes with her hand, and assumed a look of fierce concentration.

Beatriz sat down, too, dangling her legs over the edge. "Maybe I *am* from a different world," she said. "I've never met any people with wings on Earth."

"My mom says we're very special."

"Special," Beatriz repeated.

Thisby turned to her and started to say something, but cut herself off with a look of surprise. "Oh, look!

How beautiful!" She ran her forefinger along Beatriz's shoulder and gently drew it back. An emerald-green dragonfly rested on her fingertip, its wings vibrating faintly and looking remarkably like Thisby's own wings. "Look at its eyes!" They were dark red, and the facets shone with a hundred tiny points of light in the morning sun. Unnerved by the attention, the insect abruptly flew off.

"It's gone," said Beatriz. "It *was* beautiful."

She turned back to the whale. It was gone, too.

9
NASTY LITTLE CREATURES

BEATRIZ spent the rest of the morning washing her clothes and thinking about the book of spells. She borrowed a skirt from Rose that was much too long—she kept tripping over it—while her own things dried on a line strung between the wheelhouse and a flagpole on the stern.

The mysterious animal showed up again after dinner when they went up on deck to look at the sunset. It swam along peacefully beside them, and while it was still intriguing, watching it was getting a little boring, because it wasn't really doing anything. Rose scratched her cheek and wrinkled her nose. "I wonder if this isn't somebody's idea of a joke. Or maybe somebody sent it to look after us."

"Who?" asked Pyramus. "Uncle Positron? Archimedes?" Beatriz looked at Rose, but she didn't respond to the question.

The moon rose wide and yellow from behind the line of trees on the riverbank. The air was warm and smelled sweet here because, Rose said, they were farther from the ocean. One more day on the water, "if our friend here don't sink us," and they would be at Riverrun, "though the channel gets narrow. Lots of big side streams coming in. We gotta pick our way pretty careful or we'll get up one of 'em by mistake. Maybe Jumbo here can navigate for us."

She said they wouldn't need to keep watch during the night: She'd get up once or twice to check on the creature. "Though I won't be able to see the nose in front of my face after that moon goes down."

They sat dreamily watching the whale and the river and the moon until the air began to cool, and then Rose had Beatriz and the twins go below to get ready for bed while she made everything shipshape for the night.

In her cabin, a single candle next to Beatriz's bed gave off a dim, wavering light that barely reached the ceiling. She lay down and propped the photograph of her parents up on her chest. There *was* more color in their faces than before. And did they look even younger? Their expressions were also more disturbing in a way she couldn't quite put her finger on. Why didn't Rose even want to look in the book for something that might help? Maybe she already had.

Pulling the covers up close under her chin, Beatriz wondered if she ought to try praying. Death's remarks pretty much confirmed the existence of what he had called "The Big Guy." *But how do you do it?* Her family had never gone to church, except for weddings and school auctions. And wouldn't it sound phony coming from a nonbeliever? *Maybe some other time. Not tonight.* She felt oddly embarrassed.

She could hear Rose above her, moving about on deck. She liked Rose—that tough talk was just an act. Underneath it all she was a good, kind person. A good, kind person with wings.

When Beatriz woke the next morning, she had no idea what time it was. Looking out the porthole, she could see only a few feet of steely water fading into a blank gray fog. The day was quite bright, but the engine was silent, so she thought it must still be early.

Rose sat at the table in the main cabin, reading a paperback book. Beatriz noticed the faint fragrance of the spray Rose used on her wings.

"Have a muffin, kid. We ain't going anywhere till this fog lifts."

"Is the whale still out there?"

"Don't know. Can't see a blasted thing."

Beatriz picked at her muffin. Rose resumed her reading, breaking into guffaws every so often. Beatriz tried to sneak a look at the cover of her book, but Rose's hand obscured the title. All she could see was a picture of a dragon sitting at a card table, a green visor shading its eyes, dealing cards to a group of dwarves wearing party hats and smoking cigars.

She had been thinking more about the book of spells and had decided that, Rose or no Rose, today she was going to take another look at it. All morning she tried to appear lazy and sleepy, waiting for an opportunity to slip away.

The fog grew brighter as the morning wore on, until it was nearly blinding. Patches of blue appeared overhead around eleven, and by noon the last wisps of white were drifting away, leaving a clear sky. Rose said they'd get under way right after lunch, but after they had washed up, the engine refused to start.

"Dang! Condensation, I bet. Listen: You kids keep busy while I get in there and get us going. Don't want to spend the whole day just sitting here."

After asking whether he could help take apart the engine and being ignored, Pyramus found a nest of spiders under the drive shaft, and the twins began trying to herd them with a stick. After Rose wriggled in under the machinery, Beatriz left as casually as she could. She ran on tiptoe through the galley, stood a moment outside the cabin door, then very deliberately turned the handle and pushed it open.

Everything was quiet. The waves lapped at the hull, gently rocking the barge. She opened the drawer. There was the book, looking heavy and serious. Taking a deep breath, she lifted it out.

There was that tingle of electricity. She sat on the sofa and opened the cover. The dancing letters of the title page calmed as she held her hand above them. She couldn't believe she was doing this!

Okay. Table of contents. She looked down the list. Spells for making animals do your bidding, for seeing into other people's minds, for contacting the dead (she shuddered), for levitating large objects. Near the bottom she came to "'Finding Lost or Missing Persons,' page 720." After what the twins had said about not going into the back of the book, Beatriz was a little worried about such a high page number, but how could it hurt just to look?

She held her hand over the page and said solemnly, "Seven hundred twenty." Then she tried turning the page but could not. The book was like a solid block of paper. She tried saying the number in different ways: "Seven hundred and twenty," "Seven twenty," and "Seven two zero." Still nothing. Thisby had said you couldn't even get to the spells in the back—this might not work at all.

Beatriz concentrated fiercely on her hand and spread her fingers so wide they almost hurt. Very calmly, and very seriously, she said once more, "Seven hundred and twenty." With an odd feeling of strength and certainty and without any hesitation she turned the page. A dark red "720" stared up at her.

"A Spell for Finding Lost, Missing, or Misplaced Persons, to Be Undertaken with Caution" the title read. The text of the spell seemed to be in Latin, so she had no idea what it said. There was no illustration.

The sheet of blank paper lay on the left, and she picked it up and held it below the bottom of the page with the spell. What was she doing? She felt unable to resist, as if she was being pulled along by the ever-strengthening current above a waterfall. She stretched her palm out over the page. After a moment, the letters began to jiggle and jump. She let them get really excited, noticing this time a faint ringing sound like microscopic church bells clanging furiously, and brushed them down the page and onto the paper.

I should have propped it up, she thought, as some of

the little black shapes almost jiggled off the top of the page. At last they lay still in a heap in the center of the paper.

I forgot the circle! There was still the faint outline of the circle in which the twins had called up the cat, but it was smudged from having been walked on. "Thisby says it's important to have a completed circle," she told herself as if she were lecturing a child. She tried to stay calm and act in a scientific manner—and she ignored the fact that she had not at first intended actually to cast the spell.

Bending the edges of the paper up slightly and staring intently at the small pile of black letters, she walked cautiously to the dresser. She tightened her grip on the paper with one hand and let go with the other, feeling for the chalk. There it was! What a relief. Curling the two smallest fingers of one hand around it and again holding the paper in both hands, she walked back to the circle the children had drawn. Kneeling down, she let go of the page with one hand and firmly drew a new circle over the old one. After inspecting it for a few agonizing seconds and almost deciding to stop, she tipped the page up to brush the letters off—and in that moment became violently dizzy.

The letters scattered everywhere: Most fell inside the circle, but several did not. And in putting her hand down to steady herself, she smudged the chalk line.

For a second she thought nothing would happen. But of course she was wrong.

It began as a high-pitched whine, coming from near the ceiling. The corner where the walls met grew dark and fuzzy, almost as if it was filled with smoke or a little black cloud. Orange sparks began popping within the cloud, like Fourth of July sparklers. They grew brighter. The smell was now definitely smoky. Another cloud formed above the bookcase, this one with blue lights inside, and it grew brighter and larger as they popped and sparked. Then a third, on the floor near the bed—this one with green lights. It looked very sinister, sitting in a bright sunbeam.

The orange lights gathered in the center of the cloud in the corner, forming a ball about a foot in diameter, pulsing more and more brightly, gradually assuming an animal-like shape. It looked at first like a goldfish, bright orange and covered with scales. But it developed wings and legs like a bird. Then a head, which was much bigger than it should have been for a body that size. The beak was wide and sharp like an eagle's, and a horn, about half an inch long, grew out of its forehead. The color was the same brilliant orange all over, even inside its gaping mouth. It peered at Beatriz with frightful reptilian eyes and made an unpleasant gurgling noise.

She fled the cabin as a similar creature in the blue cloud uttered a high, wailing scream.

10

A CHANGE IN PLANS

BEATRIZ RAN TO THE ENGINE ROOM, yelling for Rose. The twins were still playing with the spiders, now trying to make them race one another, and Rose, beneath the engine, was swearing a blue streak.

"Oh, Rose, I've done something awful! You've got to help! I cast a spell, and something went wrong. There are these horrible things in the cabin and you've got to come *now!*"

Rose pulled herself out from under the engine and stood up, face, wings, and hands covered in oil and grease. "Geez, kid! I thought you had more sense than that. Didn't I tell you that book was nothing to fool around with? Didn't I?"

"I was just going to look at it. But I couldn't help myself. I tried the spell to find lost persons. I got dizzy when I was brushing the letters into the circle, and some of them fell out. I'm sorry. I'm so sorry."

"How many fell out? Never mind—doesn't matter. Kids, let's go. Don't get separated. And whatever you do, don't let them land on you. Fight 'em off, even if it means getting bit. They don't have teeth, but they can chew pretty hard." She rubbed her nose. Then, pulling a fire ax from the wall, she motioned for them to follow.

Even before they got to the galley, Beatriz could hear the noise, like great pieces of metal being twisted and torn, accompanied by cawing sounds—as if made by extremely hoarse crows—and something that sounded like corn being shucked, only unbelievably loud. The floor in front of them was slowly tilting down to the left.

"Holy cow! They're eating through the hull! What the heck are we going to do?" Rose stopped for a moment, then shook her head and walked grimly to the cabin door. Beatriz and the twins followed, and they all peered inside.

Beatriz hardly recognized the place. The entire side of the barge was torn away. A hole at least four feet wide, floor to ceiling, revealed the river outside—which was rapidly coming inside. The three creatures clutched at the edges of the hull, tearing off strips of inch-thick metal as if it was paper. The creatures were amazing to look at, each exactly like the others except for its brilliant color. They seemed to radiate neon orange, blue, and green.

For a moment the beasts didn't realize they were being watched. Then one looked up and screamed its shrill, gurgling cry, which made the others look around. They stared at Rose and the children malevolently. The green creature fixed on Beatriz, and its hot, hateful gaze was almost tangible, stabbing at her eyes.

Rose slammed the cabin door shut.

"Abandon ship! Sweet Christmas, we're in a fix. Let's go. Everybody astern! Move!"

"I've got to get my picture!" yelled Beatriz above the noise.

"We don't have time! We're sinking!" Rose grabbed at her, but Beatriz ducked away, ran into her cabin, and scooped up the photograph. She raced to join the others, and they scrambled along the alarmingly tilted galley floor and up the wheelhouse stairs.

"Out, out, out!" Rose shouted. "Jump! Swim for shore."

Beatriz stood for a moment on the edge of the deck, ten feet above the river, afraid she wouldn't be able to keep from going under.

"Jump!" yelled Rose, behind her.

Beatriz held the picture above her head and jumped. The cold water closed over her head—she felt as if she was being sucked down into it.

After what seemed like an eternity trying to reach the surface, she shoved the picture into the air, gasped for breath, and looked around wildly for the shore. She couldn't see it, nor could she see Rose and the twins. Without both hands free, she couldn't take off her shoes, which made it hard for her to swim. It was all she could do to tread water and hold on to the photograph. "Help! Where are you?"

There was only open water and the half-sunken barge listing crazily in front of her. Twisting around— *there* were the trees—she made her numb legs kick, and she paddled with her one free hand toward shore.

With a powerful surge that pushed her backward, an immense black object surfaced right in front of her. It was the animal—the whale. For a moment she was afraid it was going to attack her, but it just floated quietly between her and the shore. She struggled to swim around to one side, but it lifted its tail threateningly, blocking the way. She treaded water for a moment, then tried swimming around the other side. This time it let her go and followed her, a few yards behind.

She turned and sputtered, "What do you want?"

No reaction.

It took nearly five minutes of awkward paddling to get to shore. She made for a narrow, flat spot in the otherwise steep bank, a place where she thought she could scramble out. But again the animal stationed itself between her and the shore, forcing her to swim in under the canopy of a large weeping willow tree. Filtered through the leaves, the light was a beautiful luminous green, with bright little spots of it dancing over the dark surface of the water.

There was another break in the steep bank here, a flat spot nearly obscured by branches and reeds where a small stream emptied into the river, and she made for that. Struggling to her feet, she waded, dripping and shivering, into mouth of the stream, which was as warm as a bath.

"Oh, that feels good!"

She turned to see the whale—or whatever it was—unable to follow her into the shallows, floating motionless just offshore. After a few seconds it swung around and headed back to the open river.

That was weird: It herded me! I feel like one of Pyramus and Thisby's spiders!

She examined the photograph, which wasn't much damaged by the ordeal—though it was wet around the edges, under the glass of the frame—then pushed through the tall reeds and splashed up the stream through foot-deep water.

11
STONE BOWLS

THE STREAM, clear with a sandy bottom and only a few feet wide, made a tunnel through marsh grass and reeds. After following its twisting course for a dozen yards or so, Beatriz came to a small pond at the edge of the pine forest. Wisps of steam rose lazily from the water's surface.

"A hot spring!"

The air was tinged with a faint smell of sulfur, and warm water welled up around her feet. It was delicious after the chill of the river.

Setting the photograph on a mossy spot, she lay down with her head on a small mound of grass and her body angled down into the water. *Just for a minute, to warm up before I go look for Rose.* She closed her eyes and let the heat soak in. *What a disaster! I sank their boat! Oh, but that water feels so good. How could I have been so stupid? Better get up and look for Rose. But how can I face them now? I'll just lie here for another minute. . . .*

It felt as if just a few seconds had passed when she opened her eyes, but by the light she could tell it was much later in the afternoon. She had fallen asleep. The bright greens of the leaves had darkened as the sun began to set, and the air was cooler. Her stomach was complaining that it hadn't had anything to eat since lunch, and when she felt behind her with white, wrinkly fingers for her shoes, they were cold and wet.

She didn't want to get out of the pool in her wet clothes, didn't want to think about what to do next, so she just lay there, gazing up at the tendrils of steam coming off the water.

All at once she got the feeling that she was being watched. The trees were still—but she was positive there was something among them looking at her.

She sat up, heart racing. "Who's there?" She tried to make her voice sound fearless, but the words trembled. "Rose? Is that you?" Leaves rustled—didn't they? There was no breeze.

Something moved in the underbrush, coming around to her side of the pool.

She scrambled to her feet. "Who's there?" What if it was one of those awful creatures from the barge?

But it wasn't. It was a boy about her age, blond haired and scrawny, who stepped out into the waning light. He wore dark green pants, no shirt, and his hair was matted with dead leaves. A thin stick, six inches long and stripped of its bark, hung around his neck, held by a piece of brown string tied at each end. His eyes were wary, but not unfriendly. Although she had never seen him before, he looked vaguely familiar—a little like Jake from school, a boy she had kissed once on a dare and never spoken to again.

"Who are you?" he asked in a reassuringly timid voice. "What are you doing in my pond?"

"Our boat was wrecked in the river . . . and this whale? . . . guided me to the stream. I walked in."

"What do you want?"

"Nothing. I just want to find my friends."

"What happened, again?" he asked, frowning slightly. She looked down at the photograph, and he followed her gaze. "Is that your friends?"

"No. That's my mom and dad. We were going up the river to look for them. It's been acting strangely."

"What's been acting strangely?"

"The picture!" She surprised herself by snapping at him, but she was wet and getting cold in the late afternoon air, standing there explaining things.

He looked at her but didn't say anything, then turned away.

"Wait!" said Beatriz. "Don't go. I'm sorry. I didn't mean to sound like that. Please don't leave."

"It's *my* pond."

"Yes. I'm sorry. I'm lost, and it's getting dark. And I don't know where my friends are."

"The pond can tell you."

"What?"

He laughed. "The pond. It can tell you where they are."

"How?"

"You have to look at it in the right light. In the morning. I'll show you tomorrow."

"Tomorrow? But . . . I need to call somebody about my friends and the boat. Can I use your phone?"

"I don't have a phone."

"Can we go to your house? Maybe your parents . . ."

The boy looked at her oddly. "Come on. Let's go," he said finally.

A path on the other side of the pool took them into the forest. It was very narrow, winding through fir trees and around big lichen-covered boulders. The land sloped gently up, and the forest became thicker on either side as they made their way into the gathering darkness. Ferns and moss grew everywhere, even on low-hanging branches. The boy walked quickly and surely; Beatriz felt clumsy trying to keep up with him.

When they came to a wall of rocks and grass too steep to climb, the path turned to run along its base for a few yards and ended at the mouth of a cave. The boy ducked into the darkness, but Beatriz hesitated. He was fumbling around for something—after a few moments there was a flare-up as he struck a match. Then a low, steady light. She went inside.

It wasn't a very big cave, maybe fifteen feet across at its widest, twenty feet deep, and about seven feet high. The floor was hard-packed dirt, dry and level. The light came from an oil lamp sitting on a table made of sticks bound together with rope. There was a chair next to it, similarly constructed, and a ragged but clean blue-and-white-checked tablecloth. Another piece of cloth hung on the wall behind the table, and on it was a crudely drawn picture of a man wearing a panama hat. A metal filing cabinet stood against one wall, and next to that, four logs held a bed of dry leaves neatly in place.

Beatriz remembered how her father liked to wear

straw panama hats to picnics and barbecues. She gestured at the picture. "Who's that guy?"

"Dunno. Just drew him one day. For decoration, I
guess."

That seemed a little odd, but even stranger was a
collection of a dozen or so thick stone bowls, some on
the floor and others on the table. They were all about
six inches in diameter—rough textured and gray on the
sides with wide, flat rims, highly polished and deep red
in color. The "bowl" part was an indentation in the
middle only about two inches across, filled nearly to the
brim with murky liquid.

The boy carefully moved all the bowls on the table
to one side and the lamp to the center.

"Hungry?" he asked. "I'll make a fire. You can dry
off while I cook dinner."

"Are we going to eat here?" she asked.

He looked at her.

"I mean, is this some kind of fort of yours?"

"I live here."

"Don't you have a house?"

He made no reply to this and went outside. She
could hear him arranging wood for the fire.

"Great. Just great," Beatriz said under her breath.
She sat down at the table. Was he showing off, with all
the Boy Scout stuff? Why wouldn't he take her back to
his house? They had to report the accident. The cave
was cold. She hated camping.

She went out and stood in front of the fire, turning

to dry her back when her front got too hot. Soon her clothes were steaming, and shortly after that they were dry.

Dinner was a stew of some kind of dark meat, woodsy-tasting mushrooms, and potatoes.

Beatriz was impressed. "This is really good. Where'd you learn to make it?"

Again no reply.

Since there was only one chair, the boy stood next to the table while they ate from soup plates that said "Hotel Metropole" with spoons that didn't match.

"Thanks for the stew." Beatriz wiped her mouth with her finger. (No napkins.) "Uh . . . do your parents have a phone?" When he still didn't respond to her question, she asked, "What are all these?" She gestured at the stone bowls.

"That's my work."

"But what are they?"

"They're bowls. I make them. I polish them and fill them with pond water and mineral silt. They work like the pond: You can see things a long way away with them. Not as good as the pond, though."

He brought one of them over from its place by his bed and set it down reverently. It looked much the same as the others already on the table, but the top was a very deep red, and the liquid inky black, with a bright, shiny surface. "I really like how this one turned out. Look how thick this is." He dipped the handle of his spoon into the syrupy liquid and let it drip off. "I boiled it down just the right amount, so it should work really well."

"What does it do again?"

"It's easier to just show you, but it's too dark now. We'll go to the pond in the morning."

There was an awkward silence while Beatriz tried to think of something to say. "What do you do with them after you make them?"

"When I finish three or four, I leave them outside, at night, and someone takes them and leaves me food, oil, blankets—stuff I need. The good ones are worth a lot."

"Oh."

"I'm putting this one out tonight. I'm hoping I'll get a new knife. I need a new knife." He looked out the mouth of the cave at the darkness. "Sometimes I only get a bag of potatoes."

"Who—"

"I don't know." He cut her off. "They always come when I'm asleep. I've tried waiting up for them, but then they don't come."

"Oh."

He left the cave and made a few trips back and forth, bringing in armfuls of pine needles and leaves that he distributed in a roughly rectangular shape on the floor and covered with a blanket to make a bed for her.

"Have you ever been to Iowa? Or New York?" she asked.

"I've never heard of those places . . . Iowa?" He seemed amused at the sound of the word and said it several times, exaggeratedly opening and closing his mouth to pronounce it.

Geez, I hope he's not crazy, she thought.

And those bowls. The boys she knew were mostly interested in video games and basketball. If they worked at all, it was at a coffee shop or the mall. Nobody did stuff like this.

He gave her a top blanket and a coarse pillow. She undressed beneath the blanket while he carried three of the bowls outside.

She had never really given much thought to clean laundry. It just appeared in her dresser every week like magic. But it was so gross having to wear the same clothes two days in a row. She had had to do that twice in the last few days. There had to be a washing machine at Riverrun. *It must be so hard for homeless people.*

When the boy put out the lamp, she lay in the dark listening to him turning around, trying to get comfortable.

Never heard of New York? How can you not have heard of New York? The old man at the hotel had laughed when she asked if the city across the river was New York, but that could mean he *had* heard of New York and it was silly of her to think *it* was New York—or it could mean he'd never heard of New York. And Death—he only said he *thought* they were on Earth.

Where *was* she?

12

THE POND

IN THE MORNING when she woke up, Beatriz lay still, keeping her eyes closed for a few minutes, pretending she was home in bed and that the sounds of the boy making the fire and stirring a pot were the sounds of her father making breakfast. Home? Her real life? It was almost too long ago—like a story she was beginning to forget.

The bed was soft, though a little prickly from pine needles poking through the blanket. She pulled her clothes under the covers to warm them up.

The cave seemed small and dingy in the pale early-morning light. Outside, sparrows twittered, and crows cawed in the distance.

"New knife," the boy said, his body blocking the light as he came in. "And a *gallon* of lamp oil." He smiled and offered her a wooden bowl of oatmeal with brown sugar. "We've got to go soon. This is the time to see things at the pond. You have to get there before the sun gets too high or it doesn't work."

"Thanks," said Beatriz, sitting up and wrapping the blanket around herself. She took the oatmeal. "What time is it?"

"Still early."

He hadn't put any salt in the oatmeal.

"Good oatmeal," she lied. "What's your name? Mine's Beatriz."

77

He looked at the ground. "I can't tell you. I don't even know you."

"So?" It struck her that one of the first steps in getting to know someone was telling them your name.

"Eat up. Let's go."

He left the cave, and she finished her breakfast, ending up feeling full and just a little like she didn't want to go anywhere right away.

She put on her clothes, which were uncomfortably stiff from yesterday's swim in muddy water, and went outside.

Their walk to the hot spring was chilly and wetter than it had been the afternoon before. Had it rained during the night? She didn't remember hearing anything. The sun had not yet risen high enough to penetrate the trees, so the light was dim, and the air was cold and still, though increasingly filled with birdsong.

The pond, when they came to it, was surrounded by a gray mist, radiating warmth. Upwelling hot water rippled the surface, hissing quietly, churning up billowing clouds of steam.

The boy stopped by the edge of the water.

"There!" he said almost immediately. "I just saw one! Look over there!" He pointed straight ahead, through the folds of vapor.

"What? What? I don't see anything!"

"You have to look quickly. Sometimes they don't last very long."

"*What* don't last very long?"

"The things you're looking for . . . or thinking about. Everybody sees different images, but they're always in the same spot at the same time. There were a couple of deer hunters here one day, and we tested it out. Look, there's another."

This time Beatriz was looking, trying to concentrate on a mental image of her mother and dad, but all she saw was two small figures, unmistakably Pyramus and Thisby, rounding the corner of a building with a silent flurry of wings, suddenly dissolving into nothingness.

"Oh! It's them! I saw them! I saw the kids from the boat! Is this real? How do I look for my parents?"

"You've got to concentrate on who you want to see."

They stood watching the swirling mist. Trying to see her father, Beatriz got a glimpse of a forest scene, but it was only trees; there were no people. *Have to try to keep focused. Stop thinking about Rose.* The next moment she caught sight of Rose slapping her fist into an outstretched palm, mouth open in a silent roar that Beatriz knew was her yelling for the children to get their butts over here and explain some disaster or other. She smiled. "How do I know where they are?"

"You have to kind of pull back, like you're walking away from them. It takes a little practice."

She tried to picture her mom, but again all she saw were trees. *Maybe they're not close enough. Maybe they're not even here.*

She found Rose again, tried to see her surroundings,

and discovered that she could make the vision move back the way the picture does when you adjust the zoom on a camera. At first the image careened wildly in and out, like a cartoon, but after a few moments she found she could control it fairly easily. Carefully pulling back, she saw that Rose was standing by a wooden cabin near the riverbank. This quickly shrank to just a dot next to the long green snake of the river. She followed the water-course downstream and soon found a spot of white mist that she realized was the pool where she was standing. And there she was, and there was the boy! She was look-ing down, coming in closer and closer on herself, until she was looking right at her own face, and then scarily into her own enormous eyes.

"Can you see where they are?" the boy asked.

"Oh!" She shook her head. "I got distracted. I couldn't see my parents, but my friends are near the river." She felt a sense of accomplishment at how well she was able to maneuver the images and pulled back again until she could count the turns the river made between the pond and the cabin where the three fig-ures stood in a tight triangle. "Four turns up the river from where we are. There's a little house. A cabin. . . . What does it mean when you can't see something you're looking for?"

"Don't know. But your friends aren't far off."

"How do I get there?"

"I can show you the path to take. It's through a kind of a scary forest. Part of it, anyway."

Beatriz didn't like the sound of that but didn't want the boy to know it.

"I could take you there," he volunteered.

His offer was a relief, but she didn't want to seem too eager. She paused a moment before answering. "Okay. Sure. Thanks."

She watched again as Rose shook her finger at the twins, who were glancing sideways at each other, trying not to giggle.

"What do you see—when you look?" Beatriz asked the boy.

"Someone from my dreams. Sometimes I see her and sometimes I don't. Not today. It's just the quarry. Just rocks."

"Who is she?"

He didn't answer this but said simply, "It's almost over." A sheet of sunlight was coming toward them over the tops of the trees, and the visions faded as the steam grew thin in the warming air. Soon Beatriz could see nothing but the trees on the other side of the pond.

"What if Rose leaves before we get there?"

He shrugged.

They looked at each other awkwardly.

Then he said, "There are other ponds. If we lose them we might be able to find another one. Let's get some stuff for lunch at my place. It's that way anyway."

The walk from the boy's cave through the forest started out pleasantly enough. The air was cool but no longer cold, and Beatriz was well rested. The forest was full of birds, and bright sunlight soon dried the dew on the ferns and spider webs they passed. Tiny circles of light played over the tree trunks and the ground, making the underbrush almost glow.

The boy led the way and didn't talk much, mostly warning her about roots and loose rocks, asking occasionally if she needed to rest. Why should she need to rest? It was easy going. She was beginning to find him a little annoying.

After they had hiked for a couple of hours through increasingly hilly woodland, the spectacular morning had changed into an undistinguished, hazy midday. They stopped and sat on a large flat rock in the shade to eat the apples and bread the boy had brought, and to drink juice from a plastic bottle.

"What is this? It's delicious." The yellow liquid had a sweet citrus flavor that Beatriz had never tasted before.

"It's a kind of fruit. I don't know what it's called. I squeeze them by hand. They look like lemons, except they're red, and at first I thought they might be poisonous." He swirled the liquid around in the bottle. "But they're not."

It was rougher going after the break. They had to climb a series of short, steep hills, and the path was rocky and full of switchbacks. Several times they came to hilltops where there were no trees, and from one of these the boy tried to point out where they were headed.

Beatriz couldn't see anything but a seemingly endless forest stretching before them.

"I thought you said it wasn't very far," she complained.

"It'll go faster now. We're almost through the hills."

But it was another hour before they ambled down from the last ridge onto a smooth, sloping path that cut straight through a thick pine forest. Beatriz was sweaty and dusty and exhausted. *When are we going to get there? I just need to stop. Rest.*

But she didn't say anything out loud.

This forest was darker and more menacing than the bright chaotic woods on the other side of the hills. A heavy pine canopy hushed everything, cutting off the light so that no underbrush grew on the forest floor. Rows of identical trunks, mostly bare to a height of five or six feet, looked unfriendly and devoid of life. Even the boy seemed nervous.

"This the scary part?" Beatriz was a little sarcastic, trying to hide her own anxiety.

"I don't like it over here," the boy said, making no effort to conceal his. "It's not like my woods. It's creepy."

"Yeah . . . like it's watching us."

She remembered a funny movie in which—several times—someone said, "It's awfully quiet, isn't it?" and someone else said ominously, "A little *too* quiet." She couldn't remember what happened after that. This silence didn't seem funny at all. She couldn't even hear her own footfalls on the needle-strewn ground.

They hurried along the wide, level path. The sky clouded over, although she couldn't really see it through the trees, and that made the place even darker. Large mossy boulders, some as big as houses, began to appear more frequently among the trees. Soon it was so dark she could only see a short way off the path before the light faded to an impenetrable dimness.

She began to fall behind. The boy, who was walking quickly (eager, it seemed to Beatriz, to get this part of the journey over with), had to stop and wait for her every so often, obviously impatient.

Slow down! she wanted to say—but didn't. *Can't you just slow down for a minute?*

13
UNWELCOME HOSTS

THE BOY STOPPED and cocked his head to one side. Beatriz, resenting his impatience with her slow progress, caught up to him.

"What's that?" he said.

"I don't hear . . ."

"Shh!"

Beatriz could just make out the voices of several people talking, off the path on their left.

"Maybe it's your friends," the boy said.

She listened. "No, I don't think so."

Neither of them moved. The conversation was muffled but animated. Voices rose and fell, interrupted by frequent laughter. It sounded like a party, a pleasant relief from the otherwise dismal silence of the forest.

"*They're* having a good time," said Beatriz.

"Let's just keep going." The boy sounded anxious.

"No. I'm starving. They must have something to eat. And we're not going to get much farther today, anyway. It's getting dark. Maybe we can stay overnight." She didn't like the idea of sleeping in the open.

"Can you see them? I can't tell where they are."

"They can't be far. Maybe through there?" She pointed to a narrow space between two large boulders where the light was a little less gloomy. "Come on," she said. "Let's go." She walked off the path, then turned to make sure he followed her.

They had gone only a few yards before they saw a group of five adults standing around a long folding table in a small clearing ringed by giant stones and lit by paper lanterns hung from trees. They were quite dressed up: The three men had on suit coats—two wore ties—and both women wore black dresses; one even had on a pearl necklace. There were bottles of wine and platters of food on a yellow flowered tablecloth, and the partygoers nibbled off china plates and drank from long-stemmed wineglasses as they chatted. The woman wearing the necklace leaned over and began poking around in her shoe as if she was trying to clear a stone out of it.

One of the men, ruddy faced and wearing a houndstooth check sports coat and a red bow tie, spotted the children as they approached.

"Hey, there!" he bellowed. "Come on in! Plenty for everyone. The name's Bill." He strode over to them and shook the boy's hand vigorously while grinning at Beatriz. "Doris, we have visitors!"

"Fabulous." The woman, for some reason speaking sarcastically, continued feeling around in her shoe.

Why, Beatriz wondered—why in the middle of this dreary forest, miles from nowhere and really late in the day, were these people having a picnic?

The woman hiccupped and waved her hand at them. "Eat." She gestured at the table. "Food. Wine." She turned to the other two men, both of whom were watching her every move as if hypnotized. "Anyway, I *told* the man he'd better have a pretty good explanation for being there or he was going to be on his way to a deportation hearing quicker than you can say Immigration Service. And that was it. He left. I mean, he could have been after my purse or God knows what else."

"Huh," said one of the men.

"They steal from each other all the time." She turned to the boy. "Who are you?"

He blushed and stammered, "I . . . I live on the other side of the hills." He pointed toward the path.

"Do you have a phone?" asked Beatriz.

Bill laughed. "Sorry, no phone. Give you something to eat, though."

"Thank you. Can you tell me, please: Have you seen these people?" Beatriz held up her photograph.

"No. Can't say that I have. She's a cute little piece of work. He looks like kind of a slug."

"It's my mom and dad. We're looking for them."

"Here's a riddle for you: Why did the nun visit the seamstress?"

Beatriz was a bit irritated. "I'm trying to find my parents. The police are looking for them, too. We're going—" Intuition kept her from saying she thought they might be at Riverrun. "We're on our way to find them."

"Well, I suppose that's quite an adventure for you." He seemed unconcerned. "Where's the gin?"

"Who *are* these people?" the boy whispered.

Bill splashed a little gin in his glass and filled up two others halfway with something pink and fizzy.

"Try a bit of this before eating. Loosen you up. Nice little buzz—no worries. Know any riddles? Here's one: What walks on four feet—or is it three feet?—in the morning and . . . Ha! That's a classic!"

"No, thank you." Beatriz declined the glass he offered.

"Don't say I didn't ask," he said quietly. Then, "Doris, our guests aren't being very sociable. Be a dear and chat them up."

Doris, her shoe problem now apparently solved, was showing one of the other men something on the bodice of her dress. She looked at Beatriz and said, "Where are your manners? Take what's offered you and be grateful."

"Is it wine? I'm only fourteen." Beatriz thought the woman looked rather like her third grade teacher, the one everyone hated.

Bill frowned and spoke in a low voice. "It's okay to have just a little sip. Go ahead."

He made Beatriz and the boy take the glasses of the pink liquid and held up his own to toast them. "Special vintage! Cheers!"

Beatriz took a small sip. It was sickly sweet and terribly pungent, and it made her nauseous. The boy snorted some up his nose and started coughing.

"There you go." Bill laughed. "That's the real thing, eh? Here's a good one: How many barmaids does it take—"

"I think we ought to be going," said Beatriz, a little surprised at herself for saying so. But there was definitely something strange about these people, something that was beginning to set off alarm bells in her head.

˙ "Wouldn't hear of it!" said Bill. "No need to rush off." Doris held up the bottle, the pink liquid sloshing around inside.

"We've got to get back. They'll be looking for us," Beatriz lied. She felt funny. Her vision was getting blurry, and her head began to throb.

"No, no, no. Couldn't possibly let you go gallivanting off through the woods in the dark. Got to have a bite to eat, too, and you must stay the night."

"Better be going," said the boy, staggering a bit to the side.

Bill moved quickly to block their way. "Sorry. Can't let you go," he said, suddenly serious.

In the fuzzy, dizzy light the drink had given everything, Beatriz recognized what she was feeling. It had happened once before at a friend's parents' anniversary party, when she and Molly had snuck glasses of champagne. She was drunk.

The man seemed to shimmer before her. "Can't refuse our hospitality!"

"Geh away!" slurred Beatriz. "Go 'way!"

"Set you up, real comfy-like," smirked Doris.

Beatriz grew hotter and dizzier, and shortly afterward lost consciousness.

14
THE DINNER PARTY

SHE WOKE ON THE FLOOR of a dark, empty room. She was stiff and cold and, as soon as she was fully awake, filled with dread. Her photograph was gone. The boy, slumped next to her, was asleep.

She had a feeling, from the silence and a sense of closeness, that they were underground. The walls were gray plaster. There were no windows. A pale stream of cold light shone in under a rough wooden door.

She heard footsteps. She shook the boy, but he didn't respond. She stood up unsteadily, tiptoed to the door, and put her ear to it.

It was yanked open from the other side by Bill, looking seedy and somewhat scary in the harsh light of the bare bulb hanging from the ceiling behind him. Kind of like a sleazy game-show host, she thought.

"Not nice to listen at doors," he said. "That mother of yours hasn't schooled you very well."

"Who are you?"

"Oh, please. How tiresome. I believe we met last night, didn't we?" Behind him Beatriz could see a passageway lined with old wooden doors of various colors, all chipped and faded and dented. Most were obviously just nailed to the wall—as decorations?— but a few were set in doorways and had knobs and hinges. Two or three dozen black-and-white photographs were haphazardly tacked up on them, but at this distance she couldn't make out their subjects.

"You can't keep us here against our will."

"Oh, it's just for a short while. Might as well get used to it. Now, tell me if you've heard this one: Why is Beethoven like a bird cage?"

"I don't care about your riddles! Let us out of here!"

"Temper, temper! You're our guests. You'll find us decent enough hosts—if you're civil in return. If not . . ." He let his voice trail off.

She turned and closed the door in the man's face. He didn't open it again, and a few seconds later the lock clicked.

She knelt over the boy and shook him. "Hey! Wake up!"

His head flopped to the side, and he said, "Woof."

"Woof yourself. It's me. Wake up!"

"What happened?" He sat up and squinted at her. "Where are we?"

"I don't know. They got us drunk, and now we're locked up."

"Stupid people—all around us. I don't remember. . . ."

"We've got to get out of here."

She stood up and circled the darkened room, feeling the cold plaster walls to see if there was any other opening besides the door. Nothing.

She sat down. "I guess we wait. Maybe we can make a run for it when they open the door again. Bill was here a minute ago."

"What's out there?"

"A hallway. There are all these doors nailed up on the walls. And pictures on the doors. It's really weird." Where was the picture of Mom and Dad?

"A hallway? Where does it go?"

"I don't know. He didn't let me out of the room."

Neither of them spoke. They sat for five minutes . . . ten . . . longer. Once the boy grunted, "Hinges," and went over to the door to look for them, but they were on the outside.

"Isn't there some puzzle like this?" asked Beatriz. "'How did they get out of the locked room with only a block of ice and some scissors?'"

"Not you, too, with the riddles."

"Got any scissors?"

"No." He looked down. "Juice bottle." It was still tied to his belt. "Nearly empty."

"Maybe we can whack them with it?"

It was too light to use as a weapon. Even if you swung it around on its strap, you couldn't get any force behind it. They each took a gulp of juice to finish it off.

"I've really got to pee," he said.

She frowned and wished she'd eaten something when it was offered at the party.

They sat and waited. Now Beatriz had to pee.

Someone came to the door and quietly turned the key. It was one of the two other men.

"I felt bad for you," he said. "Here's a sandwich. I stole it from them—their private kitchen. It's not the party food, so there's nothing funny about it. Did you eat anything last night?"

"No," said Beatriz.

"Doesn't matter. You'll find out."

After a brief examination of the sandwich and the man, Beatriz divided the sandwich in two, and she and the boy ate hungrily.

"Can you help us get out of here?" asked Beatriz.

"Sorry, no can do. Bill and Doris run a pretty tight ship."

"Where are we?"

"A prison, really." He laughed half-heartedly. "Underground. Only one entrance, as far as I can tell. We're the 'permanent guests,' according to Bill. We spend our days down here, then drink some of the pink stuff to make us stupid and slow, and go up for dinner every night. One meal a day."

"Why?" asked the boy.

"I can't quite figure it out. It feels like they feed on our energy—what little there is of it. Like they're sucking the life out of me the whole time I'm up there. I don't know how else to describe it."

"How many of you are there?" Beatriz asked.

"How many of *us,* you mean. I think you've joined the team. From what Bill has let slip—he gets talkative when he's had a few drinks—there's normally fifteen: five for breakfast, five for lunch, and five for dinner. I've never met the breakfast or lunch crowd, and we've been down to three at dinner for a couple of months. Since . . ."

"Since what?"

The man looked away and grimaced. It took him a moment to compose himself. "Ike and Mamie were getting pretty old. Got sick at the end. And then one day, they just weren't there. Bill and Doris acted like they never had been." He looked down at his hands.

"How did you get out of your room?" the boy asked. "Can we get out, too?"

"They leave the keys in the locks—on the outside—and I smuggled down a stick and managed to push the key out of the lock and slide it under the door. Wouldn't work here. I don't think there's enough room." He bent down, but couldn't even get his little finger under their door. "And anyway, there's a big lock on the main entrance—and they don't leave the key in that one."

"How did you get here?" asked Beatriz.

He sighed. "Oh, I walked right in, just like you. I'm a logger. I was scouting a tract just north of here. And on my way home . . ." He sighed. "According to Jeanne and Tom—they're the other dinner guests—Bill and Doris actually *buy* most of their guests. Cash money. No idea who they get them from, but that's what Jeanne and Tom said. My name's Mick, by the way."

"I'm Beatriz." She looked at the boy, who looked away and said nothing. "Buy them? What do you mean, buy them? That's not legal."

"Tell me about it."

"You drank that wine and passed out, too?" the boy asked.

"I thought it was nice of them to offer. I wish I'd known." Mick sighed again. "I should have just turned and run." He shook his head and looked down at his hands again. Beatriz thought it was odd that, although his voice sounded like that of a young man, judging from his hands and face, Mick looked as if he was about fifty.

"Let me show you something." He glanced behind him and furtively pulled them into the corridor. "That's me." He indicated one of the photographs on the wall. "That's closer to what I looked like when I came here." The picture was of a much younger man. "And even that's wrong. It's changing: The guy in the picture gets older, but slower than in real life. Nothing could keep up with this, though . . . what they do to you: I'm twenty-three!"

Beatriz gasped. "How long have you been here?" The man in the photograph, while undeniably Mick, looked about thirty.

"No idea. Months? Years? Seems like forever." He paused. "Any chance of somebody coming to look for you?"

"Nobody knows where we are," said Beatriz.

The sound of a door closing came from somewhere down the hall, and Mick flinched. "Better go. See you tonight." He hustled them back into the room.

"Where's the—" Beatriz began, but he was gone, and they were locked in again. "—bathroom?"

"Well," said the boy. "At least there's only two of

them we really need to worry about. The odds have improved."

"Not by much."

"No," he said. "But he wants to escape, too. Maybe we can figure something out together."

"What about that pink stuff. It's some kind of drug."

"They're like vampires!"

A moment's silence between them stretched into minutes, then half an hour. Beatriz tried to make sense of it all, especially in light of the photographs. Were her parents "guests" here, too, part of the breakfast or lunch group? Why, in her photograph, did her mom and dad look younger than themselves, while Mick looked much older than his actual age?

Beatriz started, realizing she'd been dozing—for how long she didn't know. The boy was asleep, propped against the wall. She dropped off again after another few minutes.

They woke when Bill opened the door. He was dressed for dinner and held out a silver tray bearing two champagne glasses filled with the fizzy pink liquid.

"Champers? 'Fraid it isn't French." He winked at Beatriz.

"No, thank you," said Beatriz coldly. "Where's the bathroom?"

"You'll want a touch of this first. Just a sip."

He stood watching her until she felt forced to take

the glass and sample it. The boy did the same. Even though she took only a tiny sip, Beatriz felt the fog ooze through her body, making her limbs loose and floppy.

"So, Mick paid you a little visit, eh? Had to stand him in the corner for that, so to speak. You wouldn't like it—not like standing in the corner at home. Best to avoid it. You play fair, we play fair. *Capische?*"

Beatriz said nothing.

"Super. I just knew we were going to hit it off. But to answer your question: The bathroom's just here on the left." He beckoned her out and opened a door leading to a tiny room with a sink and toilet. The photographs on the wall outside the bathroom were black-and-white portraits—single people and couples, smiling and posing casually in a park or something. She didn't recognize anyone.

The bathroom, also peppered with pictures, was like one you'd find in a cheap, run-down restaurant. Dirty sink. Stained toilet. There was even a sign above the paper-towel dispenser that said "Employees must wash hands." It was gross, but the toilet worked, and that was all Beatriz cared about. She was shocked at her reflection in the mirror above the sink. Her clothes were smudged and pretty disgusting, and her hair was ratty. She took off her pants, rinsed her underwear in the sink—when had she last changed her underwear?—wrung them out, and put them on still damp. *Ugh.*

"I say!" Bill sounded impatient. "Everything all right in there?"

"I'll be out in a minute!"

She studied the photographs, looking for a hint of something, a clue. One of them, showing two middle-aged women, was neatly torn in half, but still tacked to the wall.

The pictures did have one thing in common with the photograph of her parents: At first glance, the smiling subjects seemed cheerful, but on closer examination, there was a disconcerting undertone, a suggestion of something wrong. There was a strange look in the people's eyes that didn't match the expressions on their faces.

"Now, on to other matters," said Bill, after both she and the boy had finished in the bathroom. He looked disdainfully at their clothes. "Not really A-list, are you? But you'll have to do." He grinned, and motioned that the children should walk ahead of him.

They wound through a maze of passageways, all of them walled with old, weathered doors dotted with photographs.

"Distinguished guests," said Bill, noticing Beatriz's interest in the pictures. "Like they have in restaurants— photos of celebrity diners. These are our celebrities." He laughed.

She tried to keep track of the left and right turns they took, but because of the pink liquor, her thinking was too fuzzy. *Have to . . . remember . . .* Beatriz couldn't think of what she needed to remember.

After a while, they came to a dead end, and a black

iron spiral staircase that led up into a dark earthen shaft.

"Onward and upward!" said Bill, shooing them up. "Here's one: Why did the exhibitionist refuse to take the elevator?"

Beatriz couldn't remember what was happening from moment to moment. She felt as if she had just been jostled awake and wasn't yet fully conscious. How long had they been climbing these stairs?

Eventually, they came to the top and to a short passage that ended at another door. Taking a ring with a dozen or so keys on it from his coat pocket, Bill opened the door, and they walked out into a cool forest evening, just where they had been the night before.

Doris, Jeanne, Tom, and Mick were standing by the table, which was again piled with food and drink. The photograph of Beatriz's parents was propped against a wine bottle.

Mick wouldn't meet their eyes. Jeanne and Tom looked tired.

"Now, then. New guests!" said Bill. "Doris, darling, will you do the honors?"

"For what we are about to receive," said Doris unenthusiastically, "we are truly thankful. Amen." Then, "Jeanne, Tom." She gestured toward the food table in a vague way. "Please serve yourselves." They silently began filling their plates. "Mick—you've done your penance. Bit of turkey?"

"Thank you, yes." He had been looking down at

the ground, but now gazed blearily at Doris, moved over to the table, and began to help himself to cold cuts and raw vegetables.

"There we go," said Bill, rubbing his hands together. "Lovely. *And* we've got our new guests!" He looked almost hungrily at the children. "What *shall* we talk about?"

"Bill!" Doris scolded. "Give them something to eat first. I'm sure they're hungry. They haven't eaten all day." She looked at Mick with mild reproach. "Except for a bit of contraband."

"Why are you keeping us here?" asked the boy angrily, slurring his words slightly. "This is illegal, you know. It's kidnapping."

"Now, now . . . be nice." Doris made a face. "This may not be like your last visit to the Plaza Hotel, but you're our guests, not our prisoners. It rather hurts our feelings to hear you say things like that."

"And we're not at our most pleasant when our feelings are hurt," Bill added. "I'm afraid . . ." he hesitated. "I'm afraid you'll have to do without your supper tonight, young man. I hate to make an example of you, but it's best to nip these things in the bud. A little more wine, however . . ." He made as if to tip an invisible glass in his hand.

"But you, my dear," Doris said to Beatriz, "you must eat something. You look absolutely famished!"

Beatriz was starving but politely said, "No, thank you."

"But you must be ravenous! Let me just get you a little something." She began picking items from the platters and arranging them on a small plate.

Beatriz heard herself speak as if she was at a distance from her own body, or was another person. "I'm sorry, I'm not really hungry."

"No, I insist. We like to think our friends appreciate our hospitality. We try to be gracious hosts, and we ask for so little in return. Hard to know what to do when guests are uncooperative."

"It's difficult for me, too," sighed Bill. "You must eat something, dear. You absolutely must." Beatriz felt that she ought to accept their offer. How bad could it be? Mick was eating.

Doris handed her the plate. There was a thick slice of turkey, and carrot sticks, and cheese on a cracker. Bill filled a glass with the pink liquid. Although she had a vague feeling that it was really something she shouldn't do, she drank another mouthful. It didn't make her feel any worse, but she was already in a stupor. She wanted to look at the boy, but a moment later forgot and began to pick at her food, wondering what she had been just about to do.

"Fantastic! I knew we'd have takers! And this looks delicious." Bill loaded up a plate for himself. "Not a terribly cheery group tonight, are we? Too bad! And on such a special occasion, too. Well, well. Natural ebb and flow, I suppose. Tomorrow's another day."

"Thanks for . . . thanks for this," said Beatriz, nodding at her plate. Then she surprised herself by saying, "Because he liked the stares?" *Where did that come from?*

"'Because he . . .' By George, you've got it! I can't believe this! Doris, did you hear? She got the elevator riddle! Why did the exhibitionist refuse to take the elevator? Because he liked the stares! Finally, a guest with some imagination!"

"It's stupid," said the boy. "What's funny about liking the stairs?"

Bill ignored the remark.

Beatriz took a mouthful of turkey. It looked fine but tasted like wet cardboard. She tried the cracker and cheese, then a carrot. Same thing. Nothing had any flavor. It was all fake, or magic—but she didn't really care. She continued to chew and swallow mechanically, then heard herself say, "And something about wanting to mend a bad habit?"

"Yes! Got that one, too! The nun and the seamstress!" said Bill. "I *am* impressed! This really is an unexpected pleasure! Here's a new one: Why did the judge put the soap-maker in prison?"

"Why?" asked the boy.

Bill looked at him quizzically. "Why, for 'lye'-ing, of course."

"Lying? Is that supposed to be a joke?"

"Soap. Lye. You use lye to make soap. Are you simple?" Bill sounded irritated. He looked at Beatriz, and she wondered what she had been trying to think of.

Bill and Doris went on to discuss whether lye was

used to make all kinds of soap or only some, though Beatriz couldn't concentrate enough on what they were saying to follow the conversation. Mick ate and drank at a steady pace, pausing between mouthfuls. After a while, he seemed to lighten up a little and even laughed at one of Bill's remarks.

When Bill and Doris had finished eating and chatting, there was an awkward silence, which Bill ended by making one of those annoying grown-up grunts of satisfaction while patting his stomach affectionately.

"Fabulous—as usual," said Doris in a bored sort of way. "Fabulous."

"Thank you, my dear." Bill turned to the boy and said in a low voice, "Unfortunate that you had to miss out on it—your own fault really—but you'll have a chance to catch up tomorrow, eh? Be in a more cooperative frame of mind by then, I'm sure. Better be! Ha, ha! Oh, here's a good one," he said to everybody. "What do an optometrist and a psychiatrist have in common?" He winked at Beatriz and smiled.

No one said anything.

Beatriz's vision was getting fuzzier. She tripped on a·root as they made their way back to the door, which was concealed beneath an overhanging rock face. The last thing she remembered, as Bill led them down the spiral staircase, was Doris saying, "She's had too much."

15

SORRY, WE HAVE TO RUN

THIS TIME, it was the boy who shook Beatriz awake. "That was so weird last night."

Beatriz sat up. She was woozy, and her head pounded. "That pink stuff. Like Mick said."

"It's like being hypnotized."

"Yeah. Geez, we've got to find a way out." She looked around the room again—it was no less a prison than it had been the day before. "What time is it?"

"No idea. Could be anything."

"That food last night was awful. Everything tasted the same. It all tasted like cardboard."

"And what's with those riddles?" The boy shook his head.

"I don't know, but he's really stuck on them."

"Yeah." He pursed his lips and frowned.

Beatriz thought for a moment. Then she said, "We can't drink it. The pink stuff. We've got to pretend. I only took a sip yesterday at first, and he didn't say anything. Or maybe we can keep it in our mouths until we get to the bathroom—then spit it out."

"What if they ask us a question or something?"

"Well, then, we'll have to swallow it." She paused. "But even if only one of us doesn't drink it, we'll be better off."

"And what if we do manage not to swallow it?"

"I don't know," said Beatriz. "But at least we'll be

able to think straight. I guess we'll have to act kind of drunk and see what happens."

They sat silently again.

They had apparently slept nearly all day because Bill, this time accompanied by both Doris and Mick, arrived shortly afterward and enacted virtually the same scene as the day before: He played the jolly host, offered them "Champers," and watched them like hawks as they went into the bathroom. Fortunately, he rattled on with his usual chatter, and Beatriz managed to keep the drink in her mouth until she could spit it into the sink. When she came out, she tried to act groggy and slow. Doris was quiet and seemed to be watching her—did she suspect something? Maybe it was just that Beatriz was more aware of what was happening around her. She hoped the boy had managed not to swallow his drink.

Bill led his "merry crew" through the passages to the staircase, collecting Jeanne and Tom from a room similar to the one Beatriz and the boy had been in, and they went up and outside.

"Chow time!" their host announced. "Why is a dog fancier like a chronometer?"

"Help yourself to the shrimp," said Doris. "Had them flown in special. Tried to get oysters, but they were all out."

Beatriz was glad to hear it.

They stood around the table, eating from a platter of pink shrimp on a bed of lettuce garnished with lemons and cocktail sauce. The shrimp looked delicious, but they tasted like more wet cardboard. Beatriz picked randomly at a slab of bread Doris had cut for her, as if she didn't quite remember what she was doing. Doris *was* watching her—she knew something was up.

Trying to act dazed, Beatriz mumbled vague remarks that made very little sense, stood unsteadily, and ate mechanically. The boy ate the tasteless food hungrily, and Beatriz thought he did a pretty good job of acting stupid.

"Still too much," said Doris to no one in particular. Were they overdoing the drunkenness? There were glasses of the pink liquid on the table, but no one asked Beatriz and the boy to drink them.

"'Oh oysters, come and walk with us. A pleasant walk, a pleasant talk . . .'" quoted Bill. "Ah! 'Why is a raven . . .'"

"'. . . like a writing desk,'" finished Beatriz dreamily, remembering it from *Alice in Wonderland*. (Or was it *Through the Looking Glass*?)

Bill looked at her with an odd expression on his face. "Yes, why? Why is it?" he asked, irritated.

She rambled a little. "Did I . . . Did . . . ?" She pretended to lose her balance momentarily, then recovered.

"Why *is* a raven like a writing desk?" Bill repeated, staring intently at Beatriz.

"Both have . . . inky quills? Black?"

"Inky . . . black . . . quills. Is that it?" Bill moved away, toward the trees, apparently lost in thought.

Doris bent down to pick up a shrimp she had dropped.

Beatriz realized this was the opportunity she'd been waiting for. She picked up one of the glasses and, as Doris stood up, threw the pink liquid in her face, grabbed her photo in one hand and the boy's hand in the other, and ran.

"No!" Bill turned and roared.

Doris sputtered and screamed, "Stop! Stop right there!"

Beatriz didn't know which way to go—it didn't matter. She just ran, skirting the boulders and trees, crashing through the underbrush. How could they lose anybody, making all this noise? The boy tripped on something and cursed. Doris's screams began to sound like those of a giant cat, yowling in heat.

"Come *on!*" yelled Beatriz.

Wind started up above the trees, making a frighteningly loud *whoosh*ing sound, and hail began to pelt the forest canopy. Doris's voice boomed out, seemingly from all around them. "Stop! Stop this instant! You can't get away from me!"

The hail dropped down on them now from the trees, blood red in color and searingly hot, hissing and burning their skin. Shielding their eyes, they ran on, skittering across a jagged chunk of ice that a few moments before had been a puddle. Beatriz crashed into a tree, almost knocking the wind out of herself, but the boy pulled her up, and they kept going.

Enormous splintering sounds came from ahead of them, like a tank smashing through the forest. "What's that awful noise?" she gasped.

They changed direction but immediately stopped short. Racing toward them in V formation were three brilliant orange creatures, identical to the ones that had destroyed Rose's boat. They flew low and fast through the rocks and trees, screeching deafeningly. The blinding light that seemed to come from their skin threw swooping, disorienting shadows all around. "I can't see!" Beatriz shouted. The creatures flew past. A careening pool of blue lights a dozen yards away veered off, too.

"Come on! Over here." She pulled the boy toward one of the gigantic boulders. They slipped into a narrow crevice that ran up the face of the rock. They would be invisible to anyone not directly in front of the crevice, since two trees blocked the view from farther away. They were sheltered from the hail, but the wind still wailed, and Doris's screams echoed throughout the forest.

Beatriz crouched down and tried to become as small as possible. The boy's eyes were closed, and he leaned against the rock, chest heaving. He slumped down after a few minutes, and they sat there, the forest raging around them, for what seemed like hours. But eventually the wind and hail tapered off, and Doris's screams, which had seemed sometimes to come from very close by, gradually moved farther and farther away.

Beatriz closed her eyes and prayed. *Thank you, who-ever you are. Thank you.* Nothing to it.

She woke in the middle of the night. The boy was asleep. The forest was silent except for the sound of water dripping from somewhere above her. She found a more comfortable position and went back to sleep.

The next morning she woke first and gently poked the boy's shoulder.

"Hey! Come on," she whispered. "Let's go."

He gave a start and looked around, frightened, before he was fully awake.

She shook her head. "What was *that* all about? Last night?"

"Don't know," he said, looking somewhat accusingly at Beatriz. "I wish you'd warned me we were going to make a run for it."

"Sorry. I hadn't really planned it. But those things? Screeching and flying around? They're what sank the boat. Tore it to pieces. I called them up from a book of spells. By mistake."

"You're the handy one, aren't you?"

"I only got three of them. There were more last night."

"Maybe they're like rabbits. You know."

"Prolific."

"That's it. 'Prolific.'" He nodded.

"Or maybe *they've* got one of those books. Bill and Doris."

"Well," he said, changing the subject, "now that you've so brilliantly engineered our escape, where do we go from here?"

She ignored the sarcasm. "Does it matter? Just farther away from those awful people."

"And which way is 'farther away'?"

Beatriz realized that, if they set out at random, they might very well walk right back to Bill and Doris.

"Listen," the boy went on, now serious. "Let's do this. We were running with the higher ground on our left, right?"

"Correct," said Beatriz.

"And we did come from that general direction, right?" He pointed.

"Yes."

"Well, assuming we didn't go around in circles, we should keep the high ground on our left and go perpendicular to the slope for a while, then head downhill—and hope we find the path. That should put us heading away from Bill and Doris."

Beatriz shrugged. "Okay." She hadn't quite followed this, but he sounded as if he knew what he was talking about. Why hadn't she taken that orienteering class at Girl Scout camp?

She went out into the open and looked around. Everything was still. The forest had an oppressive feel, but it was blessedly quiet.

They struggled along through thick underbrush for about ten minutes, then turned and went down the slope for another few minutes before coming to the path.

"Finally," said Beatriz. At least they weren't completely lost.

16

BACK TOGETHER

IT WAS A GREAT RELIEF when, after walking for an hour and a half, Beatriz noticed a new smell: the muddy, wet scent of the river. Ducks squawked in the distance. Soon she could see light through the trees ahead.

Hungry, thirsty, and dirty, they emerged from the gloom of the forest into a sunlit clearing. A cabin sat in a meadow at the edge of the broad green river. Beatriz recognized it as the one she had seen in the mists above the pond. "We're here!" She gratefully inhaled the perfume of the warm, grassy earth mixed with the heavier smells of the river.

No sign of Rose and the twins. The place seemed deserted. *Please, let them not be gone.*

The little square window set in the door was dirty and obscured by a dingy chintz curtain. Beatriz looked at the boy. He clearly expected her to knock, and she did.

There was a small explosion of cursing inside, and Beatriz broke into a smile, glad to hear Rose in her usual form.

"What the . . . ? Just a minute, I'm coming. . . . Who is it?" There was a hint of fear in Rose's voice, something Beatriz hadn't heard before, not even when the boat was sinking.

"It's me . . . Beatriz."

"Well, Sweet Baby Jupiter! Fry my wings and douse

me in hot sauce!" The door flew open, and there was Rose. She stared at the two of them for a moment before enfolding Beatriz in a hug that smelled of soap and cooking and home. For now, Beatriz forgot all about her own mom and dad and just let herself sink into the comfort and safety of a mother's arms, sobbing with relief.

Then Rose began asking where she had been and who was this grubby-looking boy, and saying how good a thing it was that they showed up, since she was just getting ready to leave. "Stop blubbering and tell me what happened, for pity's sake. We've been searching all over for you and worried sick. People from the Fish and Wildlife station—the only government up here, apparently—have been beatin' the bushes for days!"

"Can we sit down?" asked the boy.

"'Course you can. Where're my manners? Come inside and take a load off. You guys are a mess. You can wrap up in blankets, and I'll wash out your things in the sink. Hungry? I'll have something fixed up in a jiff." The cabin had two sets of bunk beds, on which they happily collapsed. Rose set a plate of biscuits on the tiny kitchen table and put a teakettle on the black potbellied stove.

It was a hunter's cabin—Rose had had to break a window to get in ("I'd leave ten bucks for them to get it fixed, if I had ten bucks"). It was well stocked with blankets and firewood and some basic nonperishable food items.

Swathed in a blanket, Beatriz told their story in bits and pieces, helped at times by the boy, as Rose washed their clothes. She made what she thought was a good argument for going back to Bill and Doris's: She was suspicious—because of all the strange photographs— that her parents were "guests" there, too.

"Oh, so that's where they are now, eh?" Rose was skeptical. "Maybe you're right, but it sounds like kind of a wild-goose chase to me. Maybe a case of 'wishing'll make it so.' I think we'd better just keep on for Riverrun. We *know* they went there."

Beatriz tried to protest, but Rose wouldn't budge. "I for one don't fancy tackling those two nasties without some firepower on our side. When we get to Jim's, we'll see if we can get in touch with somebody who knows about that kind of thing." She exhaled loudly. "Besides, we lost the barge, and I gotta make a report and notify the insurance people and all that, too."

"But if . . ."

"No *but ifs*, honey. Sorry—there's complications now the barge is gone, and even if your theory's correct, your folks'll be okay for a couple more days."

Rose changed the subject. "Let me tell the kids you're here. They've been pretty broken up about you being missing, though it hasn't stopped 'em from getting into mischief." She went to the door and yelled at the top of her voice, "PYR-a-mus . . . THIS-by . . . Come see who showed up! Yoo-hoo!"

She grinned at Beatriz and came back into the room.

"Let's see: It's going to take us at least a full day's walk to get to Riverrun—maybe longer, with the kids. With any luck we get halfway there today, after your clothes are dry. We'll sleep under the stars if we don't find another 'hotel'"—she gestured at the room around them—"and I'll make more biscuits in case we can't find a decent restaurant, ha ha. Now just where *are* those two?"

At that moment, the children came flying in the door and were all over Beatriz, nearly pulling the blanket off her in their excitement. They wanted to hear everything that had happened, and told her about their swim to shore and the long, wet walk through the forest before they found the cabin, and how they had built a signal fire that attracted a patrol boat from Fish and Wildlife.

"What happened to the book of spells?" asked Beatriz.

Rose snorted. "Bottom of the river's my guess. Good riddance."

"I'm so sorry about your boat. And the book. I was just trying . . ."

Rose cut her off. "I know, kid. You screwed up the spell *and* you sank the barge, thank you very much. The world's a genuinely exciting place when you're around. But what the hey"—she laughed a little hollowly—"nothing we can do about it now. Just promise to keep your hands to yourself from now on."

"I *promise,*" said Beatriz.

"Now"—Rose's voice took on a matter-of-fact tone—"we'll start in another hour, after I make the biscuits and we clean up the joint. Hike today, what's left of it, and get there sometime tomorrow afternoon. Can't be that far."

Pyramus complained that he had a splinter in his thumb, and Rose and Thisby went outside to perform the surgery with tweezers in the brighter light.

"You okay?" Beatriz asked the boy. He had been awfully quiet.

"They're something, aren't they?"

"What?"

"Those three."

"Well, they're a little rowdy. But they're really very nice when you get to know them."

"I guess."

17
INTO THE DARK

BEATRIZ WATCHED ROSE roll out the biscuit dough on the kitchen table. The boy had exchanged his blanket for a towel, which he wrapped around his waist, and had gone outside.

"Your friend doesn't say much, does he?" Rose asked.

"I think he's shy. He lives all alone in the woods back there."

"All alone, eh? Hmm." Rose didn't say whatever it was she was thinking, and at that moment the twins exploded into the room in a torrent of yelling and name calling.

"He took my frog! I caught it and he took it!"

"It was escaping! You let go of it!"

"I didn't! I was seeing how far it could jump!"

"Pipe down, both of you," said Rose, "Put that frog back in the water and wash your hands. I want you to come in and eat last night's biscuits while I make some new ones. And then you can help me clean the place up."

"More biscuits?" Thisby whined. "Mom . . ." But after a moment when it looked to Beatriz as if they were wondering whether it was better to fight or eat, they rushed out the door and disappeared in the direction of the river.

"Will we really get there tomorrow?" Beatriz asked.

"Well, I think so, honey. Without a map it's hard to tell exactly, but the way I figure it, we can't be more than fifteen miles off, tops. It'll be a fairly stiff hike both days."

"This forest is creepy, isn't it? I mean, I hope we don't run into anything else like those people. And we saw more of those creatures. Like on the boat."

"*That's* not good." Rose looked out the open door. "You know, it *is* strange. When I was young, we used to come up here all the time. Never saw anything like those little flying tanks. Never saw anything out of the ordinary. Wasn't so all-fired gloomy then, either." She sighed. "But everything's different when you're grown up."

Beatriz went to find the boy, hiking up her blanket to keep it from dragging in the dirt. He was sitting at the river's edge, looking at the sky, which was beginning to cloud over. Their clothes were drying on a boulder next to him, still warm from the sun. The twins were encouraging the dazed frog to jump back into the water by stomping on the ground next to it.

"What are you doing?" she asked him.

"Nothing." He looked off at the river. "I'm coming with you, right?"

"Coming with . . . ? Of course you're coming with us. You can't go back the way we came, not with Bill and Doris lying in wait like blood-sucking spiders!"

"Right." He seemed relieved.

"Rose said her friend Jim has a motorboat. He can drop you off when he takes her home. After we find my parents."

He looked out over the water, then pulled something from the pocket of his pants, now nearly dry. "Do you know what this says?"

He held out a set of keys on a ring attached to a heart-shaped pendant. Made of clear plastic, the heart was about half an inch thick and an inch across. There was a tiny crab embedded in the center, surrounded by three opalescent seashells, on a red background. Carefully inked in minute lettering, one word on each of the three shells spelled out *Tu Yo Merida*. It was her father's key ring, and her father's house keys.

Beatriz was stunned. "Where did you get these?"

"I don't know. I must've found them."

"Found them where?"

"I don't remember. Maybe in the cave?"

"They're my father's."

"How can they be?"

"I don't know, but they are."

"Take them," the boy stammered, blushing. "If they're yours. Take them. Do you know what it says?"

"It's Spanish. It's some kind of souvenir. My mother gave it to him when they went to Mexico on vacation. Before I was born. He's always had it."

"Oh. I'm sorry. I wish I . . ." He left his sentence unfinished.

"I have to show this to Rose."

Beatriz took her clothes and the keys inside and related what the boy had said.

"Hmm." Rose turned the heart over in her hands.

"Something fishy going on here. Wonder if he's mixed up in this—in your folks' disappearance."

"How?"

"I don't know. But it's kind of a coincidence he's hooked up with us, isn't it?" Rose looked at Beatriz. "We better keep an eye on him. Watch what you say when he's around."

Beatriz dressed in her clean clothes, and she and the boy, now dressed as well, chopped and carried in firewood to replace what they'd burned. Rose straightened up the cabin after the twins had straightened up the cabin, and left a note asking the owners to write to her so she could send them money for the broken window and for the food they had eaten.

"Gettin' kind of a late start, but we're on our way!" Rose was obviously trying to sound upbeat as they walked out under what was now an ominously gray sky. "With any luck there won't be any tornadoes till tomorrow." Everyone laughed halfheartedly, but the sight of the path disappearing into the cold, dark forest made Beatriz more than a little edgy.

Walking on the hard, sandy ground was easy, but it was also monotonous, since there was no variation in the forest, no birds or animals, just an endless sea of trees: gray and brown and dusty green. The boulders that so cluttered the landscape before had all but disappeared.

As she walked, Beatriz tried to come up with an explanation of why the boy had had her father's keys. It had to mean he was in some way connected to her parents' disappearance. But why would he show her the keys? Why advertise his involvement?

Having her dad's keys in her pocket, she felt she had a part of him with her, which was a surprisingly comforting feeling. But it was also unsettling, because he had lost them—or they had been taken from him.

The silence of the forest was oppressive. Rose tried to keep their spirits up with stories, but even she was affected by the gloom and eventually stopped talking, trudging along in silence.

It was the boy who kept them going, at least for a while. He seemed almost cheerful during the first hour, making a comment on one thing or another every few minutes. "I've been here before," he would say. "There's the tree with four trunks. I know I've been this far. I saw a bear here once." It was nice to know that it wasn't strange territory to all of them, but Beatriz didn't like the idea that there were bears.

A small stream joined the path, trickling down a gentle slope on their left, making a pleasant gurgling sound as it worked its way along a shallow gully. Pyramus and Thisby left the path to walk in the ankle-deep water for a few minutes, but their hearts weren't in it, and they came back up with what looked like an old chicken bone they'd found.

"C'mon, kids," said Rose wearily. "Put it down. Might have germs. Geez, I'll be glad when we're out of here. Nothing looks familiar. I used to come up here quite a lot, too." She peered down the trail. "Maybe we're north of where I remember."

Beatriz wanted a bath, and, though at home she had long ago stopped asking, she wanted her mother to brush her hair. She was going to have to remind her parents never to get lost again, when she found them.

No one said anything for at least half an hour. Beatriz watched how her feet moved as she walked, just for something to do. She was beginning to think she ought to try to make some conversation to break the oppressive silence when Rose suddenly stopped. "Now, what the . . ." She stared off to the left.

Beatriz followed Rose's gaze and noticed a blue lump that looked like a wadded-up trash bag, propped up against one of the trees a few yards off the path.

The boy picked up a stick, went over to the thing, and poked at it. It flopped over and uncurled, sprawling on the ground. It was one of the horrible flying creatures. It looked as if it had been dead for quite a while. The brilliant color had faded over most of its body to a mottled brownish-blue, and where it had been resting against the ground, white maggots writhed in the decaying flesh.

"Eeeew! It stinks!" said Pyramus.

"That's been dead for at least a week," said Rose. "So it's not one from the boat."

"What should we do?" asked Beatriz.

Rose shrugged her shoulders. "What's to do? Leave it. Keep going. Pyramus, don't touch it."

They stood around for a few moments more, staring at the pathetic little corpse. Thisby tugged at her mother's arm and said, "I'm tired. Are we almost there?"

"Almost, honey."

They went on more cautiously. Beatriz half expected one of the creatures to fly out at them from behind a tree. But it was just the same silent forest, the same dry, level path, the same gray gloom. The stream wandered off, and again nothing broke the monotony of their journey.

After another hour or so, weariness took over, and all she could think of was getting to Riverrun.

"We should have run into *somebody* by now," Rose said. "This place used to be full of people."

"Maybe those things chased everyone away," said the boy.

"When are we going to get there?" Thisby asked in a tired and soon-to-be-whining voice.

"Well, you know, kid, I'm just not really sure." Rose sounded tired, too.

They kept walking until Thisby complained again, "Mommy, it's getting dark."

It was true: The light was fading. It hadn't been noticeable at first, since the forest was so dim anyway, but now Beatriz realized it was getting late.

"We should make camp," said the boy. "This light'll go pretty fast, and we won't have time to build a fire." Beatriz didn't like the idea of staying overnight in the forest, but it didn't look like they were going to find anyplace else.

"Yep. Right you are." Rose squinted at the trees overhead. "Okay, this is the place. It's as good as any, except there's no water."

"We've still got a little left. And maybe if we look around . . ." suggested Beatriz.

Just as she said the word "around," there was a short, sharp crack from somewhere off to their left, like a big branch breaking. They all held their breath and waited, but nothing else happened.

"Mom?" said Pyramus, unable to keep a note of fear out of his voice. "What was that?"

"I don't know, honey. Probably just a raccoon." Rose took a deep breath as if she was going to shout but then exhaled slowly, saying nothing.

The boy began breaking off dead branches from the nearby trees. Everyone pitched in, and soon they had a good supply, separated according to size, with a pile of pine needles and twigs for kindling. He cleared an area on the ground, then took a silver-colored tube from his pocket. Unscrewing the top, he shook out several wooden matches.

"Now, there's our Boy Scout," said Rose. "'Be Prepared.' Isn't that what they say?"

Beatriz's anxiety began to melt at the thought of a fire.

The boy built a structure of twigs and small branches over the pine needles, struck a match, and held it under the pile until the flame caught. He blew gently into the center, and the fire came to life, crackling and sparking the dry wood, plunging the surrounding forest into near darkness. He added more and larger sticks, and soon the fire was cheerful and hot.

"Now, what about some dinner?" Rose was clearly trying to sound jolly, but it wasn't a very successful effort. "Today's special is, let me see . . . today's special is biscuits and water." The twins moaned in a sincerely tired way.

"Okay, okay. I've got some dessert, too. Everybody cleans their plate, I'll give you a lump of sugar." She pulled out six sugar cubes wrapped in white paper from her pocket.

"We don't *have* plates," said Thisby.

"Just eat your biscuits, honey. There's two each for dinner, and one more for breakfast."

"Who gets the extra sugar?" asked Pyramus.

Even though dinner was only cold biscuits and a few sips of water, everyone was glad to have stopped walking, and the fire was warm and comforting. They sat staring into it, munching in silence.

"Well, don't say I didn't warn you we might have to sleep under the stars," said Rose, "though I don't think we'll see many down here."

Beatriz said she thought they must be almost there. She had no idea if it was true. She said it just to make the twins feel better.

They were all too tired to talk much. The boy went off to gather more wood, and the others sat in silence until he came back. "This should hold us till morning," he said. "Who's taking the first shift?"

"I s'pose you're right," sighed Rose. "We'd better keep watch. Don't want any of those armor-plated birdies sneaking up on us. Or worse."

"How will we know what time it is?" asked Beatriz.

"We'll just have to estimate it, unless anybody's got a watch." She looked at Beatriz. "I had to throw mine out. Waterlogged."

"Sorry. I'll stay up all night if you want me to." Beatriz wished Rose would stop reminding her about the barge.

"Naw. I'm just teasing. We'll take turns. We'll just have to guess at how long a couple of hours is. It'll be okay."

"I found a big stick in case we need it," said the boy, brandishing a thick branch about two feet long. "For the person on guard."

"Right. Why don't you kids all get some shuteye. I'll go first," said Rose.

"When's my turn?" asked Pyramus.

"I'll wake you up for it, kiddo. Now, cuddle up with your sister and try and get some rest."

The ground was soft and covered with pine needles. Beatriz lay down opposite the boy, who sat still gazing into the fire. She rested her head on one arm so as not to get poked in the face and curled up as best she could. Her eyelids got heavy rather quickly and she found herself vaguely wondering, as she drifted off to sleep, whether sparks ever lit people's clothes on fire.

18

THE PRISONER

BEATRIZ WAS DREAMING. Her mother was holding a colander full of potatoes above their kitchen sink. The potatoes were all breathing—slowly inflating and deflating, and not all at the same time, a very odd effect.

The boy shook her shoulder and whispered, "Your turn."

Beatriz sat up, still half asleep. "What time is it?"

"I don't know. I guess about four or five. I've been up for a while. Rose is asleep."

"Anything happen?"

"No. Nothing."

"Is there more firewood?"

"There's enough. Wait until it dies down before you put more on."

"Okay." She paused. "We *are* going to get there today, right?"

"I hope so. I think it's farther than she thought." He looked over her shoulder at the forest. "This place still gives me the creeps."

"Me, too."

They were silent for a few moments, then Beatriz asked him again, "Where did you get the keys?"

"Look, I told you: I don't know. I've been trying to remember. I'd tell you if I could." He was silent for a minute, then spoke again. "I think there's something wrong with me. I can't remember anything. . . . I can't even remember my name!" Tears glistened in the corners of his eyes.

"What about your parents?" Beatriz asked. "Where are they?"

"I don't *know*. I've tried looking for them in the ponds, but I can't even remember what they look like. I must have hit my head or something."

"I'm sorry." At that moment, she truly did feel sorry for him. Not knowing where your parents were was bad enough. Not even knowing *who* they were—or who *you* were—must be even worse, if that was possible.

Unless he was just making all this up.

A breeze rustled the treetops.

"Maybe you can make up a name for yourself." She felt a little insincere saying this, as if she was playing along with his game.

"I don't want to make up a name. I want *my* name. My real name."

"Would you know it if you heard it?"

"Maybe."

She couldn't help letting a little sarcasm creep into her voice. "We can all take turns thinking of names, and maybe you'll recognize it?"

He reacted completely seriously. "No. I don't want them to know. Don't tell them."

"Okay. It's weird they haven't asked."

"I guess."

They stared into the burning coals. Beatriz always thought that Hell must look like the miniature fiery landscape inside the base of a hot wood fire. It was something to ask Death about the next time she saw him.

"I'm tired," the boy said after a few minutes. "I'm going to sleep for a while. Wake me up if you hear anything."

"Okay. G'night."

"'night."

He didn't look very sleepy, he just looked like he didn't want to talk anymore. Taking off the little stick he wore as a necklace, he wrapped the string around it and placed it carefully next to him. He met Beatriz's gaze for just a second, then lay down and closed his eyes.

Beatriz had been glad to set her photograph down after carrying it all day, but now she picked it up again and looked at it. The glass was cool and felt good against her skin, which had been overly warmed by the fire. She pressed it to her cheek for a moment. The photo itself was a little the worse for wear: river water had seeped in around the edges and stained it, and the glass had cracked in one corner, lacerating the paper. But the colors were slowly getting more intense, and her parents—her parents definitely looked even younger than before. Much younger.

She wished now she'd agreed to help organize the family photographs when her mother had asked her, years ago. They were in such disarray: hundreds of loose photos in one big box. Most of them were from her childhood, since her parents' pictures seemed to have disappeared when they moved to Des Moines after college. There were dozens of envelopes from a variety of photo labs, and a big manila envelope with hundreds of orphaned negatives. Sorting through everything had always seemed too overwhelming. Now she didn't even know where the box was—she hadn't been able to find it when the police had asked.

Standing up, and slightly dizzy from the heat, she walked a few steps away from the fire. The air was cold and smelled of pine and smoke. After her eyes adjusted to the dark, she could see a faint blue glow filtering down through the trees; there must be a moon. *If we hadn't seen that horrible dead creature or met those awful people,* she thought, *and if I wasn't starving—and if Mom and Dad were here—this would really be lovely.*

The breeze rose and fell, almost sighing. An owl glided in silence through the trees about ten yards to her left, the tops of its wings shining briefly in the moonlight. That was nice: the first real animal she'd seen except for Pyramus and Thisby's frog. She had been beginning to wonder if this wasn't like one of those nasty enchanted forests you read about in fairy tales, where the trees come alive and grab at you, or where you suddenly come on a cottage made of cookies and icing, complete with wicked witch peering out the window. More likely, she decided, the forest seemed so dead because it was contaminated by toxic waste.

She hadn't noticed it before, but there was a clearing a dozen or so yards away, where the moon shone brightly. Two large rocks sat near one another on the far side, looking like gateposts. And now, walking between them, a girl entered the clearing. She was about Beatriz's age, maybe a little older, and wore a simple shift dress that shone pale blue in the moonlight. She seemed to drift along, as if she were sleepwalking.

Beatriz stood absolutely still, watching, almost hypnotized by the girl's languid movements.

The girl came to the middle of the clearing and stopped. She looked around, seemingly confused.

Is she lost? Beatriz wondered, stealthily moving forward. When she got to the edge of the clearing, Beatriz held up her hand. The girl held hers up, too, a perplexed look on her face. She was about Beatriz's height and build, and like Beatriz had long brown hair cut with bangs.

They stood facing each other for a few moments, and then Beatriz said, "Hi. Are you okay?"

"Okay?" The girl spoke slowly and dreamily.

"You look kind of lost."

"No." The girl turned to go.

"Wait! My friends and I are camped over there—do you live around here? Do you know how much farther it is to a place called Riverrun?"

"How much farther . . . ?" the girl repeated to herself.

Hello? thought Beatriz. *Something strange going on.* "Do you live around here?" she asked again.

"We're under the bridge."

"What bridge? Where?"

"The King is there. And the Duke." The girl began to move off, back in the direction from which she had come.

"Wait. Let me get my friends. We're really hungry. Is he a real king?" But the girl was already gliding between the rocks and back into the forest.

"Wait a minute." Beatriz went after her. She thought she really ought to go get Rose first, but the girl wouldn't stop.

The girl walked slowly and deliberately down a narrow dirt road. It was very dark here: The trees were thick on either side, their branches closing overhead to block out the sky. After a short time they came to a wooden bridge, wide enough to drive a car across, the sound of a stream gurgling up pleasantly from below.

Instead of walking onto the bridge, the girl ducked under a tree limb on one side. Beatriz followed, half walking, half sliding down a brushy slope, grabbing at branches to keep from falling. At the bottom the stream was louder, echoing off the underside of the bridge. In the shelter of the span was a rough lean-to made of thick branches. A fire smoldered in front, and Beatriz could make out two lumpy figures in sleeping bags huddled at the back. A few blackened pots hung upside down on sticks pushed into the ground near the fire.

No castle for this king. Beatriz was a little disappointed, but not terribly surprised. They were just campers. Or homeless.

The girl knelt down and pushed at one of the lumpy figures. "Wake up. Somebody's here. I don't know what to do."

There were smothered sounds of irritation, but eventually the person in the sleeping bag rolled over and stared out of the lean-to at Beatriz.

"What do you want?" His voice was sleepy and hostile. "Leave us alone." He squinted into the pale darkness. "Get out of here."

The girl slumped down on another sleeping bag and watched with no apparent interest. "She followed me."

The man sat up and looked at Beatriz. "What do you want?" he demanded again, more awake now. He had a rough beard and longish hair matted from sleep and lack of washing. His grimy blue shirt was unbuttoned at the top, revealing a hairy chest and part of a tattoo.

"We're camped back by the main path. Do you know how far it is to a place called Riverrun?" A little voice inside her was getting louder, telling her to get out of there. "We have friends . . ."

"She was in the clearing," the girl broke in.

"How many did you say you was?" the man asked.

"I . . ." Beatriz had the presence of mind not to tell him how many they were. She considered running. It would take him some time to get out of that sleeping bag, and she thought she could get up to the bridge before he got going.

"Look, I don't want to bother you," she said. "I'll just go back to my friends."

"Wait a minute, kid. Wait a minute."

He nudged the other sleeping bag, and its inmate sleepily raised himself. "Whut? What's goin' on?"

"We got a visitor. I think we ought to go up and introduce ourselves to her buddies—make sure everybody's tucked in nice and cozy." He smiled. It was not at all a pleasant smile.

The other man was smaller and rounder, with dark eyes and curly blond hair. "Yeah," he said. "Okay."

The bearded man looked at the girl in the dress. "Hey, how many of 'em's up there?"

She shook her head stupidly and said nothing.

He turned to the blond man. "You gave her too much, man. Geez, just one in the morning and one at night. Is that so hard to remember?"

"Sorry, Jefe. . . . I was a little out of it myself last night. Must've forgot I'd already given her one."

That's why she's acting so strangely, thought Beatriz. *She's drugged.* Now she really was frightened. First Bill and Doris, and now this.

The black-haired man looked at Beatriz again. "What's your name?"

She hesitated for a second, then jumped up and ran.

She couldn't find the way up the slope at first, and the man yelled, "Hey, come back here! I'll catch you, kid. I can do it." She scrambled up the grade, pulling herself along by branches that scratched her hands.

He was still yelling as she ran up the road, but his voice faded quickly. He didn't seem to be coming after her.

She ran on through the clearing and back to the campfire. "Wake up, everybody, wake up! We've got to get out of here."

The boy sat up, blinking, and Rose clumsily got to her feet, still half asleep.

"What?" said Rose. "What is it?"

Beatriz tried to explain, but she was so out of breath that she could only get out a few words at a time. "I followed a girl. . . . She's with two men . . . under a bridge."

"Wait, wait, wait. Hold on there, honey. Slow down."

"Had to get away . . . had to run . . . They might be coming up here."

The boy was up, holding his little necklace like a weapon and peering into the darkness—in the wrong direction.

"Other side . . . past the clearing . . . See those rocks? There's a road through there. And a bridge. They have a thing—wood and branches. You know—a shelter."

"So they're camping out," said Rose calmly. "Like us."

"No," said Beatriz. "The girl. They were giving her drugs."

"How do you know?"

"They said so."

"Could be her medication."

Beatriz couldn't understand why Rose was being so stubborn. "No, it isn't! I could tell. We've got to do something!"

"Well, maybe when we get to a phone, we'll report it. The boys in blue can check it out if they think it's suspicious." Rose dusted the pine needles and sand off herself. "But," and here she began to sound a little less sure of herself, "maybe we ought to break camp anyway. It's nearly dawn." She had begun to look concerned at how upset Beatriz was. "Okay. Come on, let's go." She shook the twins' shoulders.

"Is it my turn to watch?" asked Pyramus.

"Maybe we should try to see what they're up to," said the boy.

"No," said Rose firmly, wrestling on her shoes. "We're just going to leave 'em be."

"But the girl!" protested Beatriz.

"I hate to have to break this to you, honey, but we're not going to sit here arguing. I'm the mom, and I say we're hitting the road. And that's the end of it." She stomped the fire out and kicked sandy dirt over it to cover the embers, then took each of the still half-asleep twins by the hand and marched to the trail, where she turned and said, "Get your butts over here, you two. Now!"

She said it the way grownups do when they really mean it, and there is nothing to do but obey. Beatriz and the boy walked after her.

19

THE COTTAGE

IT WAS JUST GETTING LIGHT, the time of day when you know the sun is coming up even if you can't yet see it. A single bird chirped sleepily in the branches overhead, and the colors of the trees and ground began to turn from the steely blue-grays of night to the soft greens and browns of the day. The walkers stopped to rest.

"Anything left to eat?" asked a bedraggled Thisby.

Rose handed the disappointed children the last of the biscuits. After watching them eat in miserable silence for a minute, she said, "You two have been real troupers. Let's do something special when we get back. Trip to the city. Restaurant, hotel, the works. Couple of movies, miniature golf, whatever you want." She didn't mention salamanders.

"Yeah, okay," said Pyramus dully. Not even the prospect of a trip to the city could revive him.

"But for now, we've still got to get to Jim's. And the only way we'll ever get there is if we get a move on."

"Hey!" The boy pointed into the woods. "There's a pond. Maybe it's like the one near my place."

"Oh! Can we look for just a minute?" Beatriz asked Rose. "It's the right time of day." Rose gave her a weary, disapproving glance but said that if they were quick, they could go ahead and try it.

The boy explained to Pyramus and Thisby how to

work the images as Beatriz stared into the warm mist rising above the water. She frowned. "We should have tried to rescue that girl. I can see her under the bridge. They're packing up to go."

"Concentrate on your mom. That's who you want to see, isn't it?" said the boy.

"I know, but I can't stop . . . oh! They slapped her, and she fell down."

Pyramus chanted quietly, "I see London, I see France . . ." Rose drew breath to say something to him when from directly above their heads one of the bright orange creatures flew at them with a horrible screech.

"Holy cats!" yelled Rose. "Don't let it get in your hair! Run!"

It came at Beatriz, claws extended, grabbing at her face. She tripped backing away from it, but recovered and ran behind a tree. It looked around stupidly for a moment, then flew off screaming toward Rose, who had had the presence of mind to pick up a thick stick. She took a good swing, but it dodged to the side and circled around for another attack.

Just as it was diving in again, Pyramus, to Beatriz's great surprise, revved up his wings until he sounded like a gigantic bee and flew straight up in the air, right between the charging beast and his mother.

"Get down!" Rose cried.

The startled creature hadn't expected the opposition to fly, and it veered wildly to one side. In the following brief moment of confusion, Rose sidestepped and whacked it directly on the head with a blow that would have knocked down a buffalo.

They stood over its seemingly lifeless form, wondering aloud if it was just stunned or if it would revive and attack them again. But it didn't move, and the orange color began to fade from its skin.

"Good Lord, I've killed it." Rose shook her head, then glared at her son. "Don't you ever do anything like that again! *You* could have been killed."

Pyramus couldn't help grinning. "Okay, Mom. Sure." She grinned back and pulled him into a big bear hug.

"Can I keep it?" he asked.

Rose gave him a dirty look. "Let's get out of here. Sun's up. Getting to be too late for the pond, anyway."

Beatriz was still staring awestruck at Pyramus but shook herself out of it and looked back at the pond. There were only a few wisps of steam over the water now. How disappointing.

They started walking again. The sun rose completely, and the forest thinned out. Dapples of sunlight splashed the ground every few yards. It would have been a nice day for a hike, Beatriz reflected, if she hadn't been so hungry and tired.

The path, which had been straight as an arrow, now curved around to the left, and they came out of the forest into a meadow of tall brown grass. A large oak tree dominated the center of the field.

Thisby pointed. "Look, there's a house under that tree!"

Beatriz hadn't seen it at first, but there it was: a small cottage, partly hidden by the thick trunk and lower branches of the tree. Following the path around to the front, they found a lovely, homey-looking place: dark brown shingles, with green trim and a slate roof—the kind of place you might see in an old photograph of your grandparents' summer house by the lake. A wall of windows with small, diamond-shaped panes ran across the front, enclosing a porch. Overgrown snapdragons and geraniums grew in a bed below, and wisteria hung from the eaves. The shiny black front door was open a few inches.

Rose knocked. "Hello? Anybody home?" No answer. A bee buzzed lazily along the row of flowers, then flew off into the field. High up in the tree, a cicada began its raspy summer whine.

"Anybody there?" Rose cautiously pushed the door open a little more. Cool air drifted out.

"Hello, hello, hello?" She stepped over the threshold. "Anybody home?" She looked back at the others.

"Can we see if there's something to eat?" asked Thisby plaintively.

"Well, I don't know. This seems a little more lived in than that hunter's cabin." There was another open door between the porch, where Rose stood listening, and the house, through which Beatriz could see a sitting room pleasantly decorated in the style favored by elderly people in old black-and-white movies: overstuffed chairs, sofas draped with white lace antimacassars, end tables with silk-shaded lamps, knickknacks and picture frames covering every available surface. Soft yellow light streamed in through the windows, making patterns on the floor.

"I feel kind of funny just barging in," said Rose, frowning.

"Mom . . . I'm hungry. . . ." Pyramus began to sniffle.

"Okay, okay, let's see what's in the kitchen." But she didn't move. "Hello!" she called out again. "We're in a bit of a fix. . . . Got some hungry kids here. We're a little lost and . . ." She paused. Still no sound. She crossed the porch, which was filled with gardening tools and supplies, and went into the parlor. The others inched in behind her.

"I don't think there's anybody here," said the boy.

"Are you kids' feet clean? I don't want you dragging in any dirt. It's a real showplace, and I'm sure cleaning these Turkey carpets ain't cheap."

"What's a Turkey carpet?" asked Pyramus.

They followed Rose gingerly into the room.

It was an interesting place, and Beatriz would have liked to spend more time looking at the pictures and bookshelves that lined the walls, and the cabinets full of objects. But they were all too hungry to think of anything but the kitchen. She did notice in passing that the pictures seemed a bit strange: moonlit landscapes with large, mythological animals racing through them; photographic portraits of people—in particular, one beautiful young woman, smiling sweetly, whose eyes seemed to glare at her. *That one's spooky. I know the eyes are supposed to follow you, but I'm sure it was frowning at me.*

After the parlor was a formal dining room, with a large table set for two: tall glass goblets, cream-colored plates with a wisteria pattern around the edge, and silverware with shiny black stones set in the handles. A single candle burned in a crystal holder in the center of the table, which could easily have seated eight.

"Well, somebody's been here not *that* long ago," said Rose, looking at the candle. "Hello!" she called out again.

Past the dining room was the kitchen, clean and tidy, with a black-and-white tile floor, butcher-block counters, and pots and pans hanging from a rack above a wood stove. Potted herbs and flowers sat on a sun-soaked ledge above the sink, giving off a pleasant smell of warm dirt and leaves.

Rose began cautiously looking through the white glass-fronted cabinets above the counters. The boy found a refrigerator in the pantry. "There's cheese in here!" he called out. "And milk and eggs and butter."

"I found bread and jam," said Beatriz. "Strawberry jam."

"All right," said Rose. "We're in business!"

She took down a frying pan, and the boy built a fire in the stove. Soon they had a big platter of scrambled eggs and cheese, with tarragon from one of the flower-pots sprinkled on top. Big glasses of milk and thick slices of bread and jam made it a real feast, and they ate ravenously.

When they had finished, and the twins had had seconds of bread and jam, Rose said, "Well, I don't know about the rest of you, but I really needed that. It's going to make the last leg a whole lot easier. I can't imagine we're all that far from Riverrun now."

While Beatriz and the boy washed up, Rose found a pencil and paper and wrote a note. The twins disappeared into the dining room.

"There," said Rose, propping the note up against an empty milk bottle. "Seems like we're making quite a habit of this."

There was a crash from the next room; the sound of breaking glass. Then silence.

"Now what?" Rose sounded exasperated. She, Beatriz, and the boy crowded through the door and confronted the twins, who were next to the table trying to look like innocent bystanders. A goblet lay shattered on the floor.

"She pulled it out of my hands!"

"I didn't! I was just trying to look at it. He was hogging it!"

"Great. Just great." Rose flushed with anger. "Listen, I don't want to hear a single word from either one of you. Get into that kitchen and find a broom and dustpan. And you," she gestured to Beatriz and the boy, "help me get the big pieces, and watch you don't cut yourselves."

Happy to be off the hook, at least temporarily, the twins ran into the kitchen.

"Dammit! I cannot let those two out of my sight for one single minute. . . ."

Beatriz noticed a subtle change in the air. She couldn't tell what it was at first, but something was happening. "Does anyone else feel . . . ?" she asked of no one in particular.

"What?" asked the boy and Rose together, but Beatriz didn't answer, and the twins came in quietly, wide-eyed. They all stared at each other.

The cottage had begun to creak and shake, the way houses sometimes do in a windstorm. But it was a sunny day, and the air outside was still, so it was a very disturbing sensation.

"What's happening?" asked the boy. "Why is it shaking?"

"It must be an earthquake," said Beatriz.

The creaking got louder, and the light dimmed. The wisteria vines outside began to wave around and curl frantically.

"They're growing! They're growing over the windows!" Rose shouted over the noise. "Let's get out of here!"

It was difficult to walk steadily through the parlor. Small items skittered off end tables, and the knick-knacks clattered in the cabinets. Beatriz had to brace herself momentarily in the doorway leading to the porch. Although the front door was open, the porch was dark; the windows and doorway were now completely overgrown with a thick mat of wisteria.

"Pull 'em down!" Rose tried to yank the vines away from the door, but they coiled around her arm, and she had to back off. "Good grief! What is going on?"

The boy picked up a shovel and started hacking at the wall of vegetation. Bright green tendrils wound menacingly up the handle, and he had to drop it.

The house shook, and the vines, curling over and around the doorway, made an unpleasant scrunching noise. They were trapped.

"Well, now we've done it," said Rose. "This is some kind of enchanted place."

"Can't we get out?" asked Thisby.

"Let's see if there's a back door."

The noise and shaking subsided as they returned to the kitchen. No back door. Rose led them on a quick tour of the rest of the house: bathroom, bedroom (*That bedspread looks just like the one on my bed at Uncle M's,* thought Beatriz), study (desk piled high with papers, and a small cardboard box filled with large glass marbles), then back again to the kitchen. No way out.

The house was quiet, but it wasn't a pleasant, lazy silence as before—it was suffocating.

"Maybe we can get out through here," suggested the boy, opening a door off the pantry and finding stairs leading downward. "But there's no light switch."

"Nooo. . . ." said Rose, peering down into the darkness. "I don't like the idea of going down there, even with that candle. Can't say exactly why, but my gut feelings are usually pretty reliable. Let's try the shovel again, now it's stopped growing." She closed the door quietly but firmly.

"Is it getting cold in here?" Beatriz shivered as a chill breeze arose seemingly out of nowhere.

"Well, it was pretty hot outside, and what with the vines and all . . ." Rose's voice trailed off as Beatriz realized that it wasn't just cool, it was actually getting quite cold, and quickly. She could see her breath.

Frost began to form on the glass of the windows and cabinets.

The boy retrieved the shovel from the porch and managed to raise the sash of one of the windows. Rose hacked at the tangle of greenery for a full thirty seconds, but it was an impossible task. She stood back, panting.

"Mom." Tears were trickling down Thisby's cheeks. "I'm freezing." Her hands were buried in her armpits for warmth.

"I know, honey. Me, too." Rose wrapped her arms around Thisby.

"What about that stove?" said the boy. "Maybe the fire's not out yet."

He blew on the still-red embers and, teeth chattering, carefully brought the fire back to life with more wood. They huddled close, hands outstretched, ears red and noses running, but at least getting warmer rather than colder.

A layer of frost so thick it resembled a light snow-fall covered every surface of the room.

No one spoke—the cold made it difficult to move their mouths.

20

ANGELA

SOMETHING WAS MOVING IN THE BASEMENT. They could hear it. Beatriz looked at the boy.

Footsteps. First on a wood floor, then slowly coming up the stairs with a heavy, deliberate tread. In spite of her fear, or perhaps because of it, all Beatriz could think of was a scene from a low-budget science fiction movie, where someone yelled, "It's coming up the stairs!" and a huge blob of goo emerged to engulf the hapless actors in ghastly green Jell-O.

But then . . . singing. A woman's voice. Beatriz didn't recognize the song, but it was pleasant, light and airy.

"At least it's not the funeral march." Rose glared at the door to the basement. It opened, and a woman came into the kitchen carrying a large tray of flowerpots. She was dressed in gauzy white tights, a short red leather skirt with a wide white vinyl belt and a fuzzy pink sweater—an interesting outfit for a woman her age, which looked to be about sixty. She didn't seem angry or surprised—indeed, she hardly seemed to notice the little group shivering by the stove.

She set the tray down, sighed, then walked over to a thermostat Beatriz was sure had not been there before and turned it up. "There we go. It's the alarm system. Very effective—when the stove's not lit." The room was suddenly warm again, and the frost disappeared.

"Now, let me see. You don't look like burglars. . . ."

"Excuse me, ma'am. We're sorry to have barged in like this," said Rose, "but we yelled for a long time and there didn't seem to be anyone home, and we were lost and the kids here hadn't had a bite to eat all day. We left a note." She picked it up and put it back down again rather lamely. Then, taking a step toward the woman, said, "Say . . . don't I know you from somewhere? You been downriver recently?"

The woman ignored the question. "Did you break something?" she asked.

"Pyramus broke a glass," said Thisby.

"*She* did it," said Pyramus.

"I didn't—"

"Hush, children," the woman said. "It doesn't matter who did it. But that's what set the alarm off. There are many valuable things in this house that I wouldn't want just walking out the door, though the wine glasses aren't among them."

"I'm real sorry," said Rose. "When we get up to Riverrun, I'll get Jim—he's the owner—to lend me some cash, and we'll pay for the damage. And the food. We ate some of your eggs and bread." She paused, and looked intently at the woman. "Didn't you take the ferry up to Riverrun a couple of weeks ago?"

"I don't know what you're talking about. But don't worry; there's no need to pay me back. You're entirely welcome." She rather pointedly took notice of Beatriz's photograph. "Dear, did you pick that up in the parlor?"

Beatriz felt the blood rush to her face and stammered that it was hers, that it was her mother and father, and that she was looking for them.

"May I see it, please?"

Beatriz showed her, keeping a firm grip on the frame. "Why, you have one of my photographs!" the woman said after a moment. "That belongs to me. I hope you weren't thinking of taking it?"

"No, it's mine! It's my mom and dad."

The woman looked annoyed. "That is *not* your mother and father."

"Do you know where they are?" Beatriz's heart was pounding.

"It *is* her mom and dad," said the boy. "Really."

"Hush! This has nothing to do with you. That picture belongs to me!" She looked at Beatriz over the top of her glasses. "You are a very rude little girl. And a thief. I will have to teach you better manners." She pulled a locket from inside her sweater, took out a pinch of powder, and threw it in Beatriz's face. *"Mortalis et verifyx . . ."*

Beatriz sneezed.

"Coriolis . . . Beatrix . . ."

"Great," moaned Rose. "Witch in a cottage. Classic."

The room began to swim before Beatriz's eyes: The walls, floor, and cabinets melted and slowly swirled around in a spiral, as if they were being stirred with a giant paint stick. She looked at her hands. The skin seemed to be oozing away from her body in a long arc.

A fuzzy gray spot appeared in the middle of the

floor. It grew to a diameter of a couple of feet and darkened, the edge sharpening to make a hole. The room was dissolving and draining down through it like water in a bathtub.

Let me see, Beatriz thought, in that detached way people sometimes have when something incomprehensible is happening. *Counterclockwise in the Northern Hemisphere, clockwise in the Southern . . . or is it the other way round?* She looked at the others. They were tall and skinny and curved, melting onto the counter top, the wall, the floor. She tried to call out, but her mouth wouldn't work.

"Ultimato exitrix . . ." the witch chanted.

The world smeared into one great dirty rainbow, and Beatriz slid into blackness.

Hmm, she thought. *This is strange. I'm still alive. Or is this what it's like to be dead?*

It was entirely dark, and she could feel nothing. She couldn't tell if she still had hands, or feet, or even eyes. She couldn't tell if she was falling, floating, or standing. Some time seemed to pass—a minute? five?—and then a pinprick of light flashed, like a lighthouse in the distance on a moonless night. She watched it grow larger, into a circle, as if she was approaching it or it was coming at her. Soon she could make out shapes inside the light: a brown oblong thing, a black lump. It was rotating—or was she going around it?—and getting closer, and at last she could make out that the brown thing was a desk, and the black lump a hooded figure sitting at the desk, working on a laptop computer. It was the per-son—being?—she had met coming out of the hallway in her Uncle's apartment building: It was Death.

I have died. She felt oddly unemotional. Not upset. More intrigued than anything else. *Maybe Mom and Dad'll be here. . . .*

She spiraled in and with a thump found herself—in her normal, everyday shape—plopped down in front of the desk, while Death continued typing, his long finger bones clacking on the keyboard. The scythe was propped precariously against a water cooler behind him.

He looked up.

"You've offended our friend Angela," he said. "The witch. And I thank you for it. She's gone and killed you! My little trap is sprung, and I've caught myself a big one!" He sounded positively gleeful.

"I'm . . . I'm dead?" Beatriz was actually a little excited at the idea. It hadn't hurt, she was still con-scious, and maybe there was a Heaven after all, with angels and harps and things.

"Well, not yet, technically. And, in fact, you won't be. In another couple of minutes I'm sending you back. Not yet 'your time,' as you know."

"So, *now* you can tell me where my parents are!"

"No, no. Sorry. Still can't do that. Confidentiality regulations, as I believe I've already mentioned."

"But that witch knows something about them. She tried to take their picture away from me."

"Maybe she does know. I'm afraid it won't do you

much good, though, with you back there and her safely in custody."

"But you can't . . . If she knows where they are, I have to find out!"

"Sorry. I don't mean to sound harsh, but we had an understanding. 'If you can manage to help me, you may possibly'—I emphasize the word *possibly*—'help yourself, too. No guarantees.' A direct quote. I have a superb memory for this sort of thing."

"That's not fair! I thought if I helped you, you were going to help me. Maybe it's not exactly what you said, but that's the way you made it sound."

Death tapped a finger on his desk and said nothing while he considered this. "Perhaps you're right. Perhaps I did make it sound a little too reciprocal." He was silent for another few seconds. "How about this: Let's say I don't take her now. Let's say I give you a week to sort it all out. But no longer."

"What happens after a week if I still haven't found them?"

"The statutes don't allow me to reacquire, after a certain point, someone I've already pronounced doomed. There's a grace period. You've got a week. Then I'm back, and she goes with me."

"Okay, it's a deal," said Beatriz reluctantly. What else could she do?

The black-robed figure snorted. "I don't do deals, my dear. This is a magnanimous gesture, one which I shall probably live to regret. Ready to go back?"

"How?"

"I just mark you 'Return to Sender' and zip you out of here. Ready? And a-one, and a-two . . ." His voice faded, and she was rushing away from the circle of light, which quickly became a pinpoint and then disappeared altogether. With a *whoosh* and a loud *pop* she seemed to fly up out of the black-and-white tile floor of the witch's kitchen. She stopped abruptly, floating about three inches in the air, then dropped down hard in front of her friends.

They stared at her.

"Where were you? And where's the witch?" asked Rose. "*She's* the one who took your folks up to River-run! I knew I'd seen her before."

"Her name's Angela," said Beatriz. "I don't know where . . ." She noticed her picture frame on the floor, the glass smashed and the photograph gone.

"She took it," said Rose, following her gaze. "She disappeared in one of those big puffs of smoke *some* people think are impressive. We figured she'd taken you with her."

"My picture..." Beatriz suddenly felt very much alone. Her renewed hope of finding her parents had somehow evaporated with the loss of the photograph.

"Hey, kid. It's just a picture. It's not going to stop us finding them. Come on—they're up at Riverrun! Don't worry about it."

"I . . . it was my only . . ." Beatriz couldn't say anything more. She hung her head, groped for Rose, and sobbed into her shoulder.

After letting Beatriz cry for a bit, gently rubbing her back the whole while, Rose said, "I think we better make tracks before our friend shows up again."

"No . . ." Beatriz began. "I've got to talk to her. She knows where they are."

"Beatriz, honey, she's definitely not the cooperative type. If your folks *aren't* up at Jim's place, we'll need to enlist some extra muscle before we talk to her again. If she does know something, somebody's going to have to make her give it up, and four kids and an old lady won't do the trick."

Beatriz looked at her hopelessly.

"We know where she lives," Rose continued. "Jim'll know who to call, once we get to Riverrun. Then we can come back, with the odds more in our favor."

Turning to the boy, she said, "Is that stove still lit? Not that really I care if her house burns down, but still . . . No? Okay, then, let's move out."

At the front door they were again confronted by the tangle of greenery. At least it wasn't growing and writhing anymore.

"Hmm," said Rose. "I'll go back for a kitchen knife. And now that I think about it, a little more grub, too, just to be on the safe side. Stay here—I'll be right back."

Beatriz pulled at a vine and stripped away a few leaves. "It doesn't seem to be in attack mode anymore."

"Hey!" The boy was staring up above the door. "Those are mine!"

Beatriz looked, and there, lined up neatly on a shelf near the ceiling, were five of the stone bowls she'd seen at the boy's cave.

"What are they doing here?" she asked. Now she was sure of it: He *was* mixed up in this somehow. "You know her, don't you?" she went on accusingly. "Do you work for her?"

He clambered up onto a wooden box. "Look! This is the one I showed you—the one I got the knife for! It's the best one I ever made!" He slid the bowl carefully off the shelf and brought it down.

"She was going to mail it," he said. The top was sealed with a plastic coffee-can lid, and an address label was taped to it, with a P.O. box return address for Angela Enterprises.

Beatriz stared at him angrily.

"She must be the one that takes them and leaves me stuff," said the boy, incredulous.

How stupid does he think I am? Beatriz wondered.

"I'm taking it," he said.

Just as he said this, a familiar voice from outside called, "Hey! Anybody home?"

"That's the man from the camp!" hissed Beatriz.

"Listen, lady," the voice went on. "It wasn't easy, but we found the girl. Let us in and pay up."

Beatriz made a face.

"Okay, then." He seemed irritated. "We'll let ourselves in." Hacking sounds. "Just clear a few of these vines out of the way." A machete blade came slicing in through the wisteria and was pulled back. More hacking—soon there was a hole big enough to see through.

"Come on," the man demanded. "We done our part. We need to get paid."

The chopping resumed, and soon the hole was big enough for him to struggle through, machete first. "Well, well. What do we have here? The mighty expedition to Riverrun."

"We were just leaving," said Beatriz haughtily, as Rose came up behind her with a bag of groceries, which she set down, and a very large knife.

"You don't want to mess with me," Rose said in a menacing voice, brandishing the knife. She pointed a finger at an empty flowerpot, which promptly exploded.

Beatriz did a double take and stared at Rose, who seemed equally surprised, though she tried to hide it.

The man said nothing, but glared at them. Rose switched the knife from one hand to the other, then back again.

"Okay, get going," he said after a short pause. "'s okay, Duke," he called to the man outside. "Let these ones go. Leave the girl out there and come on in. We got some negotiating to do with the lady of the house."

"Good luck finding her," said Beatriz as she ducked through the vines.

"What?" he began—but she was gone before he finished.

She emerged blinking in the bright sunlight. The

cottage now looked more like a compost heap than a house, covered as it was with flowers, leaves, and vines. The girl she had met in the woods was slumped over in the grass, and the blond-haired man was talking to Rose.

"There's some interesting wine glasses in there," Rose said to him. "Some of 'em's magic. We accidentally smashed one in the dining room and all this money started raining down, right out of thin air! Gold coins!"

"Gold coins?" The man looked hard at her. He didn't seem too bright.

Oh, clever Rose! thought Beatriz.

"We didn't feel right about taking 'em, of course, without asking. And nobody's home right at the moment. So we just borrowed some food. Left the money in the sideboard, in the dining room."

"Where'd you . . . ?" The man took the bag of groceries from Rose, rooted around in it for a few moments, and then, apparently satisfied it contained nothing valuable, shoved it back at her. "Nobody home, eh? Where'd you say you put the . . ."

"Duke! Get in here!"

"I'm comin', I'm comin'!" He looked over his shoulder at Rose. "Dining room, huh?" He disappeared through the wall of wisteria.

"Go get 'em, cowboy," she called after him.

They stood in silence for a minute, Beatriz watching the girl while the others listened at the door.

There was a sharp crash from inside—breaking glass—and the vines came to life, swirling and twisting and growing even more dense than before. The hole in the doorway was covered over in a matter of seconds.

"They're like worms," said Pyramus.

"Or snakes." Thisby seemed almost hypnotized.

"Good thing I put the fire out," said the boy.

"Probably so," said Rose. "Probably so. What's that thing?" She gestured at the boy's bowl.

"It's mine. She got it . . . I don't know how, but it's mine."

"Sure. Okay. Whatever you say." Rose shrugged. "But I'm not carrying it if you get tired."

Beatriz was going to have to find a way to get Rose alone, to talk about this new development. "What about her?" Beatriz looked at the girl, who seemed not to notice that anything at all was happening. "We can't just leave her."

"Yeah, s'pose you're right. And those two goons were up to no good. Let's see what she has to say."

Rose walked over to the girl and stooped down. "You okay, kid? Who are those guys in there?"

The girl shook her head.

"What's your name, honey?"

No answer.

"I think we'd better get you to a doctor. You don't look so good."

The girl stood up and began walking away. "Where you going?" Rose called after her.

Beatriz ran to catch up with her. "Those men are . . ." She didn't know what to say. "You should come with us. We'll help you."

The girl stopped and seemed to be thinking. When she turned to Beatriz, tears were streaming down her face.

"It's okay. Come with us." Beatriz put an arm around her shoulder and guided her back to the others.

"Another mouth to feed," said Rose, but she, too, put an arm around the girl. "It's okay, honey. It's gonna be okay."

21
RIVERRUN

THEIR PROGRESS WAS SLOWER NOW. The girl wouldn't—
or couldn't—walk very fast. Beatriz stayed with her
when she fell behind, hoping Rose would fall back, too,
so they could talk without the boy overhearing them.
But Rose stayed in front with him and the twins.

They *had* to be getting close to Riverrun. Beatriz
clung to the hope, implausible as it now seemed, that
they would round a bend and find her mom and dad
sitting in the shade by the river, surrounded by the
staples of an old-fashioned summer camp: lodge, boathouse, cabins, laughter, and canoes. It wasn't such a
strange thing to hope for; Death had all but said they
were still alive. And maybe the witch had left them at
Riverrun for some reason. She stared at the boy's back,
angry because she couldn't get him to tell her about his
involvement with the witch and what, if anything, he
knew about her parents.

In the late afternoon she smelled the river again. It
was faint at first, mixing with the hot scent of pine needles and dust, but a mossy muddiness gradually over-
powered the dry forest smell, and soon she could see
blue sky on their right: the edge of the forest—and the
river.

The path now ran alongside the river for the most
part, retreating briefly into the forest only when there
was an impassible stretch of riverbank. The river here

was faster—and much smaller: you could almost throw a stone across it. Near the edge the current swirled through brown shallows and spread in smooth sheets over wide, flat rocks. The middle of the channel was still deep enough for large boats, but navigating the barge through it would have been tricky.

Rose made the others stop, to let Beatriz and the girl catch up.

"Any chance of you telling us some details about yourself, kid?" she asked the girl. "How you hooked up with those two guys? It might help us figure out what to do with you."

The girl thought for a moment, then shook her head. "I don't know. . . ."

"Looks like you've been through a lot. Sometimes it's good to talk."

The girl said nothing.

"Okay. Maybe later."

The air by the river was refreshing, and Beatriz felt that now they really must be nearly there.

And indeed, after another fifteen minutes or so they passed a small wooden sign reading RIVERRUN—.5 KM, and shortly after that they came to the place itself.

It wasn't what Beatriz had expected. Just a couple of rundown outbuildings—one was a boathouse with a chipped and faded RIVERRUN INN & RESORT painted on the side—and a big white clapboard house that had seen better days. The lawn, stretching from the house down to the water, hadn't been mowed in several weeks and badly needed weeding for dandelions. A row of aspens and a low stone wall marked it off from a meadow, and the forest lay beyond that. Spreading maple trees shaded everything—a nice change from the pines and firs of the forest. Cicadas buzzed lazily high up in the trees.

The day was now hot. It was the sort of afternoon when you don't want to move around any more than is necessary.

No sign of Mom and Dad. Beatriz knew it hadn't been very realistic to expect them to be right there, but she was disappointed that they weren't. Maybe inside . . .

"Hey, Jim!" Rose yelled toward the house. "Jim! It's Rosie!"

There was a clatter inside the boathouse, and then, "Hello? Hello?" The door opened, and a man with tousled gray hair and round black-rimmed glasses came out, wiping his hands on an oily rag and grinning.

"Is that the Rose who's a Rose who's a Rose? And what others sniff the air as sweetly beside you? Proud Pyramus and young Thisby!" He smelled of gasoline and whiskey. "And twice as many more!" He smiled at the three others as he gave Rose a hug. "Hooked up with the Gang of Four Plus One, have you?"

Rose playfully pushed him away. "Kids, I want you to meet my good friend Jim. Always a guaranteed entertainment. Jim, this is Beatriz—she's why we're up here to see you—and these are mystery kids we picked up along the way. I don't even know what to call 'em. Of course, you know the Dynamic Duo."

"Don't know what to call 'em? How about we call 'em in for iced tea and cookies? Leo's probably got something about to boil inside, besides his temper. It's tax time, so at the very least he's cooking the books."

Beatriz tried to interrupt politely. "Excuse me. Do you have some guests staying here, a man and woman? They came up by boat with an older lady?"

Jim laughed. "Nobody here now. It's getting to be a bit late in the season."

"They're my parents. I think a witch—the lady who was with them—kidnapped them and sold them to some people in the woods."

"Beatriz, honey," said Rose, "why don't we get in out of the sun and have a sit-down, and you can tell him the whole story. My feet are killing me."

"I don't want to hear the whole story *again,*" complained Pyramus.

"In we go, little mice." Jim shooed them toward the house. "I'll give you a hook on which to hang your tale, missy, and we'll listen to its end."

"Excuse me?" said Beatriz.

"Let me take your coats," he said. But as they hadn't any coats, she just let herself be herded toward the house. Rose smiled at her and shrugged.

The house was a rambling three-story affair, reminding Beatriz of what you might see in an older section of Des Moines. A wide wooden stairway led up to an enormous railed porch that curved around the front of the house and extended along one side, a porch populated by clusters of white wicker armchairs with fat green cushions. A glider, a sort of sofa-on-a-swing, with cushions that matched those on the chairs, stood near the wall at the front entrance.

The screen door banged shut behind them, ushering them into a reception area, cool and airy, with sunlight from tall white-curtained windows glancing off the polished dark wood of the floor. An elaborately banistered staircase rose up on the left, at the foot of which stood a coat rack (no coats) and a spindly wooden table supporting the guest register. The walls were papered in a green floral pattern bursting with pink and red blossoms.

Heading down a hall toward the back of the house, they passed a living room with a wide stone fireplace that squatted cold and dark below a mirror-crowned mantelpiece, the focus of several overstuffed armchairs and a bright yellow sofa. In the dining room, at the end of the hall, a cut-glass chandelier illuminated a large oval table covered with piles of manila folders and papers.

"Blast!" said Rose. "My tax audit's next Tuesday! I was counting on spending the rest of this week getting ready. I'm going to be in such hot water!"

"Defy them! No quarter given!" said Jim. "Hot water is for tea, not taxes."

They went through a swinging door into the

kitchen, which smelled warm and cakey. A short, round man, bald and sweaty, was wrestling with a stack of papers at the kitchen table and looked up when they entered. Beatriz liked him instantly.

"Leo, I smell something half-baked in here," Jim announced. "Fix us some tea, there's a good soul. Weary travelers pine for tea!"

"Pine for tea . . . pine for tea . . . hmm . . ." Leo considered this for a moment. "There's a joke in there somewhere. Anyway, the kettle's on—it'll be ready in a minute. Sorry the place is such a mess. I'm having a go at the taxes. Deep in the heart of 'em."

He rose to give the twins' mother a hug, and Jim introduced everyone else. With a theatrical sigh of weariness, the boy set his stone bowl down on the floor next to the stove and pulled off the plastic lid to inspect it. He had carried it alone and without complaint all day, and Beatriz felt a twinge of guilt for not having offered to help.

Everyone arranged themselves at the table while Leo scurried around, clearing the papers out of the way, filling a pitcher with ice cubes, making the tea, and finally producing a platter of freshly baked ladyfingers.

When what seemed like a decent interval had passed, Beatriz again asked about the young couple with the older woman and gave an abbreviated version of her story.

"Hmm," said Leo. "Not sure I remember them. Let's check the register."

Beatriz and he excused themselves, retrieved the guest book, and took it into the living room. A brass clock under a glass dome on the mantel ticked quietly. Beatriz jumped a little when it chimed the quarter-hour.

Leo tilted his head back to see better as he ran his finger down the pages. He hogged the book the way adults often do, and although Beatriz didn't want to get too close to him—he smelled of sweat and yeast—she leaned over his shoulder to see if she could recognize her father's handwriting.

There seemed to have been an awful lot of guests in the past few weeks.

Leo looked thoughtful and tapped the book with his finger. "H. Does it start with an H? Harris? Harley?"

"Harry! My dad's name is Harry! Do you remember him?"

"Is that him?"

Her eyes fell on the unmistakable signature of her father. It was a party of three, and they had signed in nearly three weeks ago.

"That's him! And my mom! And the old lady—the witch?—that's Angela. Do you remember them? Do you know where they were going?"

"Young couple, older woman, right? I think we gave 'em the top two rooms, in the attic. Too hot in midsummer, but they're nice enough now." He consulted the register again. "They only stayed three days. Didn't say where they were going. Not that I remember, anyway."

"Can you remember *anything* about them?"

He looked thoughtful. "I liked the young woman—kind of a wistful type. The old lady was a pill. I'm not surprised to hear she's a witch. Her bed was too hard, her eggs were never right, the tea was always too weak. She dressed kind of peculiarly, too."

"Can we show this to Jim? Maybe he'll remember something."

Sadly, Jim couldn't remember them at all. "Wasn't that the week I was doing all the end-of-season work in the boathouse?"

"You're always 'working' in the boathouse," said Leo hotly. "I think that's why you *dis*-remember so much."

Beatriz broke the uncomfortable silence that followed this remark. "Has anyone stayed in that room since? Maybe my parents left something? A receipt, a note? We might be able to figure out where they were going."

Leo scanned the register. "Room's been empty since they were here, but Jim would've cleaned it long ago."

"Ah," said Jim, rather pointedly. "Seems to me that when we decided to put the acrobats on the second floor, I might have, uh, postponed the housekeeping on the top floor." Leo glared at him. "But now, aren't you glad I did? Up, up, up!" Jim jumped to his feet. "Let's investigate. Nothing like a mystery to top off teatime!"

"You kids stay with me," Rose said to the others. "No sense everybody tromping all over the clues. Pass the ladyfingers, please."

Beatriz and the two men went upstairs.

The second story was quiet; a thick green carpet runner muffled their footsteps. At the far end of the hall a smaller, less grand staircase led up to the attic.

The anteroom at the top was hot and stuffy, its ceiling sloping down to meet the floor on one side. There was a door in the wall on the other side, and one straight ahead. A tattered fishing magazine adorned the seat of a lonely-looking chair.

"The old lady had the single, and the other two were in this one." Leo nodded at the door in front of them.

He turned the knob and pushed it open.

It was a pleasant little room: two single beds with patchwork quilts, a duck decoy made into a lamp on a small writing table, two green wooden chairs. The low walls were papered in a subdued floral pattern and the ceiling angled up steeply on each side to the peak. A single window looked out over the lawn to the river.

"It reminds me of the rooms in Mr. Borges's hotel," said Beatriz.

"Borges!" exclaimed Jim. "Fabulous! A little cuckoo now, but we're all prisoners of the clock in the end."

Beatriz looked around. Not much to see. She sat on one of the beds. "Is there a bathroom?"

"Just through there." Leo pointed to a small pine-panel door.

She went over and looked in. Used water glass. Soap

wrapper on the sink. Bits of wood shavings and brown string in a blue plastic wastebasket. *Wood shavings?*

"What about the other room?" she asked.

The room where the witch had stayed was equally bare. She'd even made her bed.

They went back downstairs in silence.

22

ENTR'ACTE

"ANY LUCK?" asked Rose.

"Nothing," said Leo. Then, looking at Jim, "Don't forget to clean it."

"Tomorrow morning, bright and early. First thing."

No one spoke for a few moments. Beatriz was near to tears. This had turned into a dead end.

"The little blue wastebasket," said the girl, speaking for the first time since they'd arrived. "With the flower decal."

Everyone stared at her.

She seemed startled. "What? What did I say?"

"You said 'the little blue wastebasket,'" said Beatriz. "There *was* one. In the room. How did you know?"

"I—I . . . don't. It just came out. I'm sorry."

"Have you been upstairs?" asked Rose. "I don't think so."

"No. Once. I don't know."

"Not a bad guess," said Jim. "But *all* the wastebaskets are blue." He gestured at a stack of them, in the corner, nearly obscured by a pile of old newspapers.

"Oh," said the girl. "I must have seen them."

That put an end to the discussion, but it was an odd remark, coming out of nowhere like that. Beatriz watched the girl for a minute, trying to figure something out—she didn't know quite what—while the others went on talking.

"What to do? What to do?" said Jim, shaking his head.

"On to Plan B," said Rose. "But is that back to the witch, or back to the party people?"

"It doesn't matter." Beatriz sighed melodramatically.

Rose ignored this. "Either way, we're going to need help."

"We'll need professional advice," said Leo. "OSHA, don't you think?"

"OSHA!" said Rose. "Great idea."

"Who's Osha?" Beatriz asked.

"OSHA's not a 'who,' " said Jim. "It's a 'what.' A government agency: Office of Sorcery and Hex Abatement. They handle cases of deliberate misuse— abuse, really—of magic. Only the serious stuff. They have an agent working out of the Fish and Wildlife station up here. Couple of ticks down the river."

"What's 'ticks'?" asked Pyramus.

"Can we get hold of them?" asked Rose.

"Nothing's easier," said Jim. "I'll take the motorboat. Be back in half an hour."

After he left, everyone sat silently at the kitchen table, the twins fiddling with their forks and the others watching them. Beatriz finally went into the living room to be alone and flopped down on the sofa. She closed her eyes and tried not to think.

Why weren't her parents here? They were *supposed* to be here.

When Jim returned, he said that the agent was out

for the day but would come by at ten thirty the next morning. "Looks like we're in for a little weather, too," he said. "Wind's picking up. Might rain before tomorrow."

"Can he . . . can the agent make her tell us where they are?" asked Beatriz.

"Don't know." Jim shrugged. "We'll have to see."

"And in the meantime," said Leo, "there's no sense just sitting here. You two," he nodded at the older boy and girl, "help me clean up the tea things, and the rest can give Jim a hand to make sure there are enough rooms made up for tonight."

After changing the sheets on a couple of beds, Beatriz finally had a long, hot bath, which made her quite sleepy and somewhat less despairing. There was, after all, a plan, and they were going ahead with it. She dressed in the clean clothes that Jim found for her— they had a good supply of things left behind by forgetful guests.

When she came downstairs, Leo was just putting dinner on the table. The kitchen was full of people and steamy smells from a deliciously aromatic chicken stew seasoned with bay and rosemary.

"Just in time!" said Leo, setting down a big porcelain tureen in the center of the table. "Soup's on."

After dinner Leo made a fire in the living room, and they all found things to read: third-rate mystery stories, well-worn magazines about "country living," several years old—mediocre items Jim and Leo didn't much mind the resort's guests walking off with. Beatriz took her father's keys out of her pocket and looked again at the little scene in the plastic heart, as if there might be a clue embedded in it along with the seashells and the crab.

"Do you know what this says?" she asked Jim.

"Hmm. Possibly. I don't recognize the specific language, but the roots suggest 'You' on one of the shells and 'Me' on the other. 'Merida' on the third . . . I don't know what 'Merida' is."

"It's a city. In Mexico. My parents went there once."

"It's like what you would carve on a tree with a sweetheart," said Leo. "Like 'Molly loves Leo' in a heart with an arrow through it."

"Oh." Beatriz suppressed a pang of sadness. She put away the keys when she noticed the girl watching her.

Complaining that there was nothing to do, Pyramus found a pencil and began poking at a blue tropical fish in a small aquarium until Rose told him to stop. She gave him a deck of cards, and he and Thisby played a game that involved eventually forcing one's opponent to take all fifty-two cards and hold them in one hand.

After about an hour the boy, who had sat in silence the entire time, said he wanted to go to bed, and Jim took him and the girl upstairs to their rooms.

"Time for you two to hit the hay, too." Rose patted Pyramus on the shoulder.

He was concentrating hard on the card game and only grunted, but Thisby stood up and said, "I'm tired."

Beatriz and Leo were the last to go up. He gave her a sympathetic look and said, "Not to worry. We'll get it figured out. Those OSHA people are sharp as chickens."

"Chickens?"

"I mean 'sharp as a tack.'" She could tell that he was trying to make her feel better by joking. "Seriously, they know their stuff. They'll know what to do."

In her room she changed into a nice clean night-shirt, several sizes too large. She took her father's keys out of her pants pocket again and set them on a table next to the bed. How familiar they were, shiny and silver and brass, with the little red heart she had never really looked at closely before yesterday. Now they assumed an importance they never had for her in Iowa.

She hadn't really thought her mom and dad would be here. Well, yes, she had. But she couldn't give up now. This was just a setback. They had found the witch, which was important. And it sounded as if the OSHA people were the reinforcements Rose thought they needed to deal with her.

But what was so special about her mom and dad that Angela should want to kidnap them in the first place, if that's what she had done? How could Angela even *know* them?

After turning out the light, Beatriz snuggled down under the covers and listened to the rising gusts of wind, accompanied now by spatters of rain on the window. The lights left on in the kitchen and living room cast an intersecting patchwork of rectangles and parallelograms on the ceiling. How far away she was from her room at home and from the bedroom at her uncle's, with its branchy shadows on the ceiling. She began counting the rectangles of light but fell asleep long before she finished.

23

REVELATION

IN HER DREAM, Beatriz was fishing with her dad. They were in a rowboat on a very still lake. It was early; the light was pale and the water perfectly smooth, unruffled by morning breezes. A heavy mist surrounded them, and she could see the trees on shore only intermittently.

Her dad put down his fishing pole and reached into his pocket. "How many times do I have to give these to you?" He smiled and passed Beatriz his keys, on the key ring with the little red plastic heart. "You can let yourself in."

She took them silently and put them in her own pocket. Just then there was a tug on her line.

"Okay . . . stay calm," her father said. "Don't jerk the rod. Let him bite a little more solidly, then pull back—but not too hard."

Big bite. The rod jerked her shoulders forward. It happened again.

"You've got him!" said her dad. "Now you've got him!"

"Dad! What do I do? It's—"

"Beatriz! Hey, come on." His voice sounded strange. "Wake up! Rose says to come down to break-fast."

"What?" Still half asleep, she opened her eyes to see her father looking down at her, shaking her by the shoulder. No, wait—it wasn't her father. It was the boy.

He was talking to her. "It's late and the guy from whatever-it-is is supposed to be here soon. Rose says to come down. They saved you some breakfast." He turned and left the room.

She rolled onto her side and looked out the window, disoriented by the transition from the dream to wakefulness. The rain, coming down steadily, splashed on the first-floor roof just below her window and snaked in little rivulets to the gutter. The wind had stopped.

She really had thought it had been her dad waking her up. Something in the boy's eyes. Something she had seen in the photograph of her parents that the witch had taken from her, something that remained of her father in spite of the disturbing aspects of the picture.

He was getting younger in the photograph.

The boy had her father's keys.

And in the dream . . .

She sat bolt upright, heart pounding.

Suddenly everything was clear. The boy wasn't helping her look for her father, he *was* her father! He *was* mixed up with the witch, but not in the way she suspected. Angela had put him under some kind of spell. And she had made him younger, so of course he didn't know his own daughter: His life as a father hadn't *happened* yet.

Angela had wanted the photograph back because she didn't want Beatriz to see his likeness eventually change to match his enchanted appearance. Like Bill and Doris's picture of a younger Mick, it took a while for the images to catch up with the person's actual age.

Beatriz dressed quickly and ran downstairs.

Yes! Now that she looked at the boy—how could she have missed it? The way he stood, the way he held his shoulders, his face. Everything! Even the wooden stick he wore around his neck: the wood shavings in the wastebasket upstairs, the brown string! "Dad! It's you!"

He backed away. "What? What are you talking about?"

"The witch has you under some kind of spell to make you younger, to make you forget!"

"Whoa, whoa, whoa," said Rose. "What's all this?"

Beatriz stumbled through her reasoning for the grownups. Pyramus and Thisby stared at her, fascinated.

"That's a very interesting theory," said Leo slowly when she had finished. "I don't know if I buy it, but I bet the OSHA agent will have an opinion. How handy that he happens to be coming by this morning."

"I *know* it's true," said Beatriz, looking at her father. "It *has* to be. I can *see* it!"

But now the thing she had seen in the boy's eyes as he leaned over her this morning was gone, replaced by a look of anger, a fierce look she had never seen in her father's eyes.

"It's why you don't remember anything!" she insisted. "Not your name, not how long you've been here, not anything! You thought you hit your head, but you didn't—she did it to make you forget!"

The boy stared at her defiantly.

He doesn't know it's me. This was even worse than not having known where he was.

How can he be my dad if he's my age? She felt abandoned. Her real father was gone and there was only this dorky *kid.*

Nothing to hold on to. She was a bird, blown about in a windstorm.

How could he do *this to me?*

For some reason, she remembered him telling her about his twentieth high-school reunion—the only one he'd ever gone to—and how at first he didn't recognize anybody. After a beer and about half an hour, he said he'd recognized *everybody,* but they all looked as if they'd been inflated, like balloons—some more than others. Here it was just the reverse. He looked as if he'd had the air sucked out of him. He was so skinny, and his skin was so smooth. But it was *him,* and he didn't know who she was!

"Hello, hello?" A voice came from the front of the hotel. "Anybody home? Aloysius Waddle here. Northern District OSHA."

"Yo!" chorused Jim and Leo.

Rose pulled open the kitchen door, and a little man who looked more like an accountant than a magician scuttled into the room. He wore a tan raincoat and a brown fedora protected from the rain by a plastic bag,

and he carried a black leather briefcase. Pulling a carelessly knotted yellow necktie from beneath his coat, he
dabbed at the water on his cherubic face and looked
around at them curiously.

Beatriz slumped into a chair. She couldn't think. It
was all just too much. She stared at the boy, who turned
away from her.

"Now, what seems to be the problem?" asked the
man, shaking the water off his hat.

"Well," said Rose, "we've got a witch and some
slave traders and now there's this young man." She nodded in his direction. "Can you tell if he's under some
kind of enchantment? Like one that made him younger
by, say, thirty years?"

"Ha!" the OSHA man said. "De-aging. Nasty
business."

"Harry." The girl they had rescued looked at
Beatriz's father. "You're Harry."

The boy glared at her. "No. I'm—I'm not." He
sounded unsure.

He recognizes his name!

Beatriz looked at the girl, and a wave of vertigo passed
through her. She felt as if she was looking down at the
kitchen from a great height. Now that she had seen her
father in the boy, it was almost hilariously obvious that
this strange, abused girl was her mother! Her face, her ges-
tures, the photograph, the blue wastebasket, everything. It
was the same effect: She looked as if she had had the air
sucked out of her. But her eyes, her mouth, her hands!

"Mom!" Beatriz wanted to throw her arms around her, but a look of utter bewilderment on the girl's face stopped her.

I've found them! Both of them! They were with me all the time. But it isn't them. They're children!

She backed away and sat down, not knowing what to do. *Why is everybody just sitting around talking? Why don't they change them back?*

"Please! One thing at a time!" The OSHA agent appeared flustered. "Now, this boy ... thirty years younger, you say?" He looked around the room, then settled on Leo with an accusatory stare. "And is there a suspect?"

"Uh . . ." Jim fumbled for a moment, obviously confused. "We're pretty sure it's a witch. Brought 'em here a couple weeks back, before he ... before *they* were fully . . . young, un-grown, you know. But they can't remember."

"Naturally. And somebody's going to be in a whole heap of trouble," said the man, still regarding Leo with suspicion.

Stop it! Stop talking and just fix it! Beatriz closed her eyes. She could hear the blood rushing in her ears.

"Don't look at *me.*" Leo sounded as if he were getting ready for a fight. "I'm the proprietor of this establishment. We're trying to help."

"Ha!" exclaimed the agent. And then "Ha!" again, a little less vigorously, now regarding the stove with suspicion. Then "Hmm." He circled the boy and the girl, looking them up and down.

"What?" said the boy. "I haven't done anything."

Beatriz opened her eyes. Everything was still the same. They were still children.

"Didn't say you had, didn't say you had." The man's voice was kinder. "Just trying to get a fix on things. Get a bead, so to speak."

He turned on his heel, flipped his briefcase onto the table with a flourish, and produced a sheaf of papers, which he thrust at Rose. "If you don't mind getting started on these . . ."

She riffled through them and looked at Jim. "Good practice for my audit, I guess. There's ten pages of forms to fill out here."

"Only seven," said the OSHA agent, sounding slightly peeved. "But we need complete documentation before I can begin. If what you say is true, this isn't a parlor trick we're dealing with here. It's serious business."

And as he opened his mouth to add something to this, a familiar voice came from the dining room: "You can't even begin to know *how* serious it is, you little twit!"—and Angela the witch entered the kitchen, trembling with rage. She would have been comical, in her short skirt, fuzzy pink sweater, and white tights if she hadn't looked so menacing. Seeing Beatriz, she snarled, "You! I thought I'd gotten rid of you, you interfering little girl! *This* time I won't be so careless!"

"*You* did it!" Beatriz shouted. "You changed them so they wouldn't remember! Change them back!"

"Ahem," the OSHA agent interrupted. "Are you indeed responsible for this enchantment?"

"What's it to you, shorty?" Angela glared at Agent Waddle.

"Change them back!" Now it was Beatriz who was shaking with anger.

"Madame," the OSHA agent said to Angela, "I'm afraid I'm going to have to ask you . . ."

"Don't you 'madame' me, pal. And stop interrupting!" She stamped her foot like a petulant child and turned to Beatriz again. "Now I find out that you had my book. And then *lost* it. You *idiot!*"

"Your book?" Rose sounded confused. "You're not talking about that book of spells, are you?"

"Yes, I'm talking about *my* book of spells, and I'm talking about her running off with *my* stoneworker." She looked at the boy. *"And* I'm talking about losing a ten thousand–dollar bounty for a fresh, young guest for my client's dinner parties. I had to hire detectives to get her back, and look where she's turned up!"

The agent interrupted again. "Ahem. Pursuant to section 4485 of the criminal code, I'm placing you—"

"You're not placing anything! *You're* just one step away from being toast!" The witch jerked the locket from her neck and raised it above her head. The chain skittered across the floor.

"Toast? Did you say 'toast'?" Clearly the OSHA agent didn't understand.

"Look out!" Beatriz cried. She ran for the door, and the others followed. Nine people tried to squeeze through, all at the same time. Beatriz and the twins got out first, followed by Rose, the boy, and the girl. Jim, Leo, and the man from OSHA were last.

The agent backed out through the door, holding up his hands in a "Let's not get all worked up" gesture, saying, "Now, listen, my good woman . . ."

But Angela was having none of it. Beatriz turned just in time to see her point a finger at him and, with her other hand, whack the side of her head. A ball of blue flame shot from the witch's fingertip and engulfed the three men. When it subsided, there was only a swirling pile of ash on the dining-room floor.

Everyone else crowded down the hall toward the front door, but Angela materialized in front of them with a great roaring sound, blocking the way. "I'm not finished with you!" she cried, taking a pinch of powder from her locket and flinging it at Beatriz.

Beatriz managed to dodge most of it, but a few grains stuck to her face, and the room began to swirl in the same whirlpool way it had back at the witch's cottage. She turned and staggered into the living room, wiping her face with her hand and smearing the powder on the back of the sofa. The dizziness stopped, but the sofa began vibrating violently.

No way out. She shoved her way into a closet full of heavy overcoats and pulled the door closed behind her. It was pitch black and smelled of mothballs and something awful, like a dead fish. She hoped she wasn't going to sneeze.

A cold hand touched her shoulder. She jumped. A bare light bulb went on overhead, illuminating the figure of Death, nicely concealed among the coats.

Beatriz was relieved. "Oh, it's you. I'm *so* glad to see you."

"Now *that's* a first," he said. "I must say, you've certainly got her in a lather."

"I have no idea . . ." Beatriz began.

"Nothing you could have done differently. Hair-trigger personality."

"But . . . did you come to take her? It hasn't been a week yet, and I found them, but they've been enchanted into children!"

"Technically, our agreement was that you had a week to find your parents, which it appears you've done. But don't worry. I just happened to be passing by and thought I'd check in on you. Things going well, overall?"

Beatriz laughed despairingly.

He continued, "Normally, I don't like to say 'I told you so,' but you *do* see what's happened because I gave you that extra week, don't you? Those gentlemen she dustified a few minutes ago make three additional wrongful terminations. And then there are the two ruffians she turned into squirrels back at her cottage because they bungled their so-called detective assignment. Guess who gets to do the paperwork on all this?"

"Can we talk about this later? She's going to do something terrible to my mom and dad, and Rose, and . . ."

Beep!

Death pulled out a cell phone and consulted the screen. "Hmm. Sorry to say I must fly. There's an event at a fireworks factory I can't miss. Yet another reincarnation of Attila the Hun. That man *cannot* keep out of trouble. And of course the Big Guy wants me to handle it personally."

"But what about the witch?"

"You're on your own for the moment, I'm afraid." The beeping resumed. "The fireworks have already started—at the factory, I mean—and they do their work pretty quickly. I'll be back as soon as I can. In the meantime, you'll be safe in here. She can't get in—I'll make it invisible from the outside." He backed through the tightly packed coats and disappeared.

24

ALONE

BEATRIZ STOOD STILL, feeling the house shake every few seconds with great crashes coming from outside. It sounded as if huge boulders were raining down. Had Angela blasted Rose and the children the way she had blasted Jim and Leo?

She opened the door partway and leaned out a few inches, listening intently. The living room was deserted; the noise was coming from other parts of the house. Now it sounded as if enormous trees were being splintered upstairs. Angela screamed—from the kitchen?—and Rose—yes, that was Rose's voice—shouted something Beatriz couldn't make out.

She opened the door a little wider. Empty room, smell of smoke and sulfur. The hallway was illuminated by flickers of red and yellow light, and occasional bright blue flashes. A cautious step out. "Maybe if I can get them in here with me . . ." Checking behind her to make sure the door stayed open, she found only the flat surface of the wall. The closet had vanished.

The noise was incredible. And through a window she could see flames licking the outside walls. The witch was ranting in the kitchen, though Beatriz couldn't hear what she was saying.

Sneaking up to the kitchen door, she tried to peer through the crack, but just as she got close enough to see, the shock wave from a clap of thunder many times louder than anything she'd ever heard blew the door open and slammed it into her face. A simultaneous burst of blue light was so brilliant that she was momentarily blinded, and she stumbled to the floor.

Then silence. Complete silence, except for a high-pitched ringing in her ears.

Sprawled on the floor, forehead throbbing painfully, she was too dazed to move. She had no feeling in her nose, but after gingerly touching her face all over, she discovered that at least she wasn't bleeding.

The kitchen door had swung closed, and everything was still, except for the ticking of the clock in the living room.

After a few moments she managed to stand up, somewhat unsteadily. Her head pounded, and she felt as if she was going to throw up. It was so quiet. What had happened?

Outside, the rain had stopped, and sunshine bathed the bright green lawn in a sparkling, gold light. A robin flew down to the grass from a maple tree and hopped around, looking for something to eat.

Beatriz pushed the kitchen door open. Nothing. No one there. The power seemed to have gone off— the electric wall clock had stopped. The breakfast dishes, half washed, sat beside the sink. A spice rack had been blasted from its place on the wall and lay shattered on the floor, giving off an oddly appealing smell of hot glass and burnt lavender.

Beatriz dabbed at her nose with a damp dish towel. She was relieved not to see any more piles of ash. Where was everybody?

Poor Jim and Leo. And that other man. She went into the dining room to look for the ashes that had been her hosts and inverted a cereal bowl over them.

"Rose?" she called out. "Rose, are you here? Anybody?"

She went through the house and then out onto the porch. "Rose! Where are you?"

Nothing. A swallow darted out from under the eaves of the boathouse, skimming across the river, looking for insects.

She sat down on the glider and gave a push with her foot to set it swinging.

What to do? What to do? Jim had said that. No help from him now.

Where was everybody? Where were her mom and dad?

A ladybug made its way along the glider's armrest. When it got to the end, it paused for a moment, then opened its wings and flew away.

She went inside and found the stairs leading to the basement. Taking a flashlight from the kitchen, she somewhat nervously went down to look for the circuit breakers, to try to get the power back on. She couldn't find them, but she did find a root cellar lined with rough wooden shelves, and canning jars full of tomatoes and pickles neatly arranged in dusty rows. She had missed breakfast in all the excitement, so she took a jar of tomatoes upstairs, popped the seal, and carried it out to the porch. She held it just under her chin and spooned up the sweet red flesh, delicious and smelling faintly of basil, until the jar was half empty.

Okay. Got to think of something.

She searched the house and grounds, hoping to find a clue as to what had happened, to where everyone had gone—for *anything* that would suggest a course of action. The house was a mess, especially the second floor, which seemed to have borne the brunt of the damage, but that was all it was: just a mess. No clues, nothing useful. She ended up sitting on the porch again, still at a loss.

She considered taking the motorboat down the river to the Fish and Wildlife station, but when she went out to the boathouse to look at it, it was too big and complicated. She decided that she would wait until the next morning and take one of the canoes. It was already midafternoon and seemed too late to start off, especially not knowing exactly where she was going. The current would be with her, and she hoped it wouldn't take too long to get "a couple of ticks" down the river.

When it began to get dark, she went into the living room to build a fire. The little blue tropical fish, so lively the night before when Pyramus was chasing it with a pencil, floated dead at the top of its tank. With no power, the air pump had stopped.

Beatriz was overcome. "Oh . . . you poor thing. I'm so, so sorry." Of course it wasn't her fault, but she felt that somehow it was.

She built a fire and sat on the sofa, staring into it for a long time, until it was reduced to embers and she couldn't keep her eyes open anymore. Covering herself with an afghan that was draped over the back of the sofa, she curled up and went to sleep.

She woke up hungry and shivering early the next morning. The sun had just begun to rise over the trees on the far side of the river, and it cast big orange rectangles on the wall opposite the windows. Her face felt almost normal.

Need to heat water for tea. Wrapping the afghan around her, she shuffled into the kitchen. She could see her breath. She turned on the oven and opened the door to warm up the room. *What's for breakfast?* Oatmeal. She dropped raisins into boiling water to soften them before adding the oat flakes. Standing in front of the oven, stirring the cereal, she began to thaw out a little.

Her foot bumped against the boy's stone bowl.

Of course! The bowl! Why hadn't she tried it yesterday?

A wisp of steam floated up from the central depression, above the silt and pond-water mixture.

She picked it up gently and took it to the table. The sides were slightly warm from the heat of the stove. Bending down so as to be level with the top of it, she waited for a moment, then saw the steam rise again. There was Thisby! Her face was tear-stained and miserable. And Mick, the logger—Bill and Doris's prisoner.

She concentrated and tried to pull back to see where he was. Yes . . . there was the hallway with the doors covered with photographs. And there was Bill, talking to Rose, who looked very upset. Her wings were creased and drooping. She was frowning and speaking angrily.

At least they're alive.

A part of her felt she ought to stick to her original plan and paddle down to the Fish and Wildlife station, but how long would it take to get them to do anything? How many forms would she have to fill out? And what might happen in the meantime?

No. She would go by herself—now—to Bill and Doris's.

After bolting down her tea and oatmeal, she threw some bread and a chunk of Swiss cheese into a cloth shoulder bag and found a plastic bottle she could use for water. She debated whether to take the stone bowl but in the end decided not to. It was too heavy, and besides, now that she knew where everyone was, there was really no need for it. She headed out the door and down the path.

25
THE SECOND PHOTOGRAPH

FROM THE SAFETY OF THE FOREST'S EDGE, Beatriz surveyed the witch's cottage. Everything looked normal: The flowers in front waved slightly in the breeze, a yellow butterfly glided past the black front door, and other insects—wasps?—swarmed around a spot under the eaves, from which hung an entirely reasonable amount of wisteria. The only sound was from the grasshoppers whirring through the dry grass of the meadow.

Now she wished she'd taken a more careful look with the boy's bowl. Rose and the twins were with Bill and Doris, but what if her parents were here, with Angela?

Should she skirt the meadow and keep going? Or try to see if there was anyone in the cottage?

She waited five minutes. Nothing moved except the top branches of the oak, when a breeze came up briefly. She crouched down and scuttled into the meadow, along the path to the cottage. Pressing herself against the wall next to one of the parlor windows, she edged over until she could see inside. No lights on. Photographs and knickknacks all in place. She started when her eye fell on the photograph of the young woman—the one she thought had glared at her the first time she was here. It still seemed to be looking right at her, scowling. Was it Angela, when she was younger?

She went around the back and crept up to the

kitchen window. Nothing there, either. Just the row of flowerpots on the windowsill, everything neat and clean. Circling around the house, she peered through gauzy curtains into a deserted bedroom, opened the door of a musty tool shed (shovels, spiders), and investigated a chicken coop set some distance from the cottage.

There was a wooden enclosure in the coop, and a roofed area for the chickens to run in, but . . . nobody home. Putting her fingers through the chicken wire, which tingled faintly, as if weakly electrified, she clucked softly. "Here, chick, chick, chick. Here, chicky."

A high-pitched shriek made her jump back just in time to avoid one of the horrible blue creatures. It flew out of the enclosure straight at her and crashed into the chicken wire where her hand had been a moment before. Two more, both orange, followed the first. As she stood a few feet back, paralyzed by the shock of the encounter, they clawed at the fencing, screeching and trying to grab at her.

"Wow," was all she could say. "Wow!" She backed farther off. *Does Angela raise them?*

She continued around to the front of the house, heart still racing.

Standing with her hand on the doorknob, trying to summon up the courage to turn it, she heard a scrabbling noise in the branches overhead and looked up.

Oh, please don't let them be in the trees, too.

An acorn hit her shoulder, and two big red squirrels raced to the top of the tree, chattering loudly.

Turning the knob, she quietly stepped into the porch. Absolute stillness.

What if Angela was in the cellar? She tiptoed through the parlor and silently opened the door in the pantry that led downstairs. No sound. Nothing.

Not here. Maybe with Bill and Doris?

She relaxed a little, and since the house seemed deserted, she decided to explore the rest of the rooms. In the parlor she picked up the photograph of the young woman and examined it closely. The face was angry when you stared into the eyes, but when you looked at the whole picture, the woman was smiling winsomely, almost flirtatiously, at the camera.

This is *Angela. I know it is.*

She slipped the picture out of its frame. It felt faintly electric in her hands, as the book of spells and the chicken coop fence both had. On the back, faded writing, in pencil: "Graduation, Bridgeport." Did that name sound familiar?

What is it with these pictures?

She put the photograph in her shoulder bag. *Angela was right. I am a thief.*

She poked around in the bedroom closet, which was filled with silly clothes that looked as if they came from a Halloween shop, and examined the cardboard box of glass marbles she had seen on the desk in the study the first time she was in the cottage. It contained about a dozen loose marbles, all about an inch in diameter and perfectly colorless, and a single marble that nestled on a bed of blue velvet inside a small plastic case emblazoned with a gold triangle. A warning label on the bottom of the case read, "Always wear protective eyewear. Angela Enterprises takes no responsibility for unprotected viewing." There was a pair of dark industrial goggles next to the box.

She put them on and took the marble out of its case. It was light but definitely made of glass, not plastic. Perfectly spherical and without any bubbles or flaws, it felt slippery, though the surface was dry. She held it up to the light and looked into it, but immediately shuddered and looked away. She couldn't remember afterward what she had seen that was so unpleasant, but she had no desire to look twice.

She moved the box to one side to look at a blueprint beneath it. The triangle logo was printed in one corner, above some indecipherable text. And there was a drawing of a sphere, with mysterious symbols in the margins connecting to various points on its surface. "Orb of ~~Immobillity~~ ~~Imobbillity~~ ~~Transfixtur~~ Stops Them Dead in Their Tracks!" was scribbled on a Post-It note below the logo. *That sounds useful,* she thought. She popped the case into her bag and left the cottage.

She walked for hours, passing the place where they had been attacked by one of the orange creatures (it was much too late in the day to think of trying to see anything in the pond); the place where they had camped and found the girl; the place where they had seen the dead blue creature. The forest, too, seemed dead. Just endless dusty green trees, mile after mile. Had it been this desolate before? She'd had company then, and it hadn't seemed quite this bleak. At least there weren't any mosquitoes.

It was beginning to get dark. How much farther? She tried to add up the time it had taken them to get from Bill and Doris's to Riverrun, just the walking part, and came up with a disheartening twelve or thirteen hours. She wasn't going to make it in one day. Which might be just as well, since she thought she'd rather arrive during daylight anyway.

If she could just get to the hunter's cabin. But even that was a long way off.

Spending the night alone in the forest was not something she wanted to do, so she kept walking, nervously, taking a break for a bit of bread and cheese every hour or so. There was enough moonlight for her to see the path, which glowed like a grayish-blue ribbon beneath the trees. The air was completely still. She was tired, but having had a couple of days of good meals and sleep, she had the strength to fight off exhaustion. *Girl Scout camp . . . ha! Piece of cake.*

At last she came to the clearing where the hunter's cabin stood, dark and unwelcoming, but a sight she was grateful for. She didn't bother to knock. Flopping down on a bunk bed without washing her face or taking off her clothes, she fell asleep instantly.

26
TAKING A CHANCE

BEATRIZ WOKE in what felt like early afternoon, made a face at her bedraggled self in a mirror near the sink, and went out to the river to rinse off the previous day's dirt and grime. A bubble bath. *That* was what she really wanted: a nice hot bubble bath. At home. In the bathtub.

She took off her clothes, rinsed her socks and underwear, wrung them out as best she could, and laid them on top of a boulder to dry. Wading into the shallows, she dunked her head several times and sat down to wash her feet, face, and hands.

"Ow!" The sharp corner of a rock poked into her leg. Feeling around in the muddy water, she discovered it wasn't a rock, it was . . . a piece of wood? She pushed it, and it moved a little, though still stuck in the soft bottom. It wasn't wood, unless it was covered in . . . rubber? She dug into the ooze and tried to pry it out. After she had worked at it for a minute, the river gave up, and a book came out in her hands, its wet green leather glistening in the sun. It was *the* book. The Book of Spells.

She held it gingerly, unable to believe it had found her. Because that had to be what had happened. It had presumably sunk with the boat a long way downstream and couldn't possibly have found its way up here if it had been an ordinary book. Which of course it wasn't.

She took it into the cabin and left it on the table

while retrieving her damp clothes from outside. By the time she finished dressing, the book was perfectly dry and showed no signs of having been in the water for . . . how long? At least a week.

She sat down and opened it to the table of contents.

She closed it again. What was she doing? Last time she opened it "just to look," she ended up casting a spell that went horribly wrong. *Have to think about this first.* She *had* promised Rose she wouldn't fool around with it, but it was such a powerful tool . . .

She opened it again.

"About Cats." "Finding Lost or Missing Persons." "Conjuring an Invisible Asp." "Forcing Rhinoceri to Do Your Bidding." *Hmmm. Definitely don't want to fool around with* that *one.*

"Moving Large Objects Through the Air." Maybe she could squash Angela with a boulder.

"A Sword of Invincibility." *Oh, come on! How about a Bazooka of Invincibility?*

"A Spell for the Protection of Persons or Animals." That sounded promising. Could she protect her parents with that? No harm trying. If it didn't work, they'd be no worse off than they were now. Wait. What was she thinking? She hadn't prepared the circle or anything.

Prepare the circle? She didn't even want to cast a spell—she just wanted to look! She closed the book again firmly. She wasn't going to let herself be seduced into doing something rash.

Chalk. Is there any chalk around here?

A bit of burned wood from the stove made a nice, black circle in the middle of the table. *I hope the color isn't important,* she thought, *especially it's being black and all.*

She opened the book and found the spell again in the table of contents. Fairly close to the middle of the book, so maybe not as dangerous as the last one. And look, how handy, a small illustration of the boy and the girl who were her enchanted parents! But . . . no sheet of blank paper. How was she going to brush the letters off the page?

Not seeing anything else nearby that she could use, she pulled Angela's photograph out of her bag and held it below the book. The letters danced and bounced under her outstretched palm, and she carefully brushed them onto the face in the photograph, making sure not to spill any. Sitting down at the table slowly and putting her feet apart for stability, she brushed the letters off the photograph and into the circle.

The moment of dizziness passed quickly, and that was it. Nothing else. The little pile of letters gradually lost their color, like the cat, and disappeared.

Well, I suppose nothing really does happen if you're protecting someone. That's the whole idea. She felt glad she'd at least tried it—and hadn't botched anything in any obvious way.

The photograph seemed unaffected, but when she looked into the eyes, the face was one of absolute fury and almost unbearable pain. It shocked her so much she jumped. *Back in the bag with you, lady!*

27
DEATH, WHERE IS THY STING?

BEATRIZ WRAPPED THE BOOK in a towel and hid it under a pile of brush behind the cabin. She didn't want to take it to Bill and Doris's and risk letting Angela get her hands on it.

And it's not the sort of thing you can use with people whizzing around attacking you.

There was still a small lump of cheese in her bag. She took a bite, gave a final look around, and walked out the door.

It was only an hour and a half's walk to the place where she and the boy had left the path and found Bill and Doris's dinner party. The "dining area" was deserted. On the table were a stack of dirty plates, a few glasses, and a half-empty bottle of the pink liquid. The yellow tablecloth was stained brown in spots, and the strings of paper lanterns hung limply, looking tired and worn. It all seemed rather small and shoddy in the daylight. She found the door leading underground and tried the handle. Locked.

She explored the woods around the clearing, looking for another door, and for a stick she could use as a weapon. Why hadn't she brought a kitchen knife or something? How could she take on the witch and Bill and Doris with a stupid stick, anyway?

No, she couldn't take them on in a fight. What else? She couldn't think what she could do to trick them. Maybe she should go back and get the book.

Or maybe she should go find the Fish and Wildlife people and let OSHA deal with the situation.

But what, exactly, *was* the situation? *What if there isn't anybody here? What if they've gone somewhere else?*

She decided to wait until dinnertime to see if anyone showed up.

She found a hiding place behind a large fallen tree just a short way from the door. There was a gap between the tree and the ground at one spot, through which she could see the table in the clearing.

Then she waited. Hours passed. An uncomfortable thought crossed her mind: What if the witch could see through the eyes in the photograph and knew what she was up to? That might explain the strange changes of expression.

Well, of course it was possible. *But what about when it's in the shoulder bag? And wouldn't she have already come to get me if she knew where I was?*

At last the sun began to set. Beatriz realized she had been dozing for . . . how long? It must have been a while. She stood and shook her arms and legs to fight the creeping chill. Then, lying down on the mossy ground, she peered into the clearing. *They* have *gone somewhere else. I'm waiting for nothing.*

Nothing happened for about ten minutes more. Then . . . the lights in the paper lanterns came on.

Now she was fully awake and watchful.

She couldn't see the door without standing up, but a minute later she heard it click. There was movement, and

Doris came into the clearing, toting a pair of grocery bags. She tied up the dirty dishes in the old tablecloth, put the bundle on the ground, and spread out a new cloth. After unpacking clean plates and glasses, she laid out the food: cold cuts and vegetables, a nice-looking pie, a casserole covered in tinfoil. And two more bottles of the pink wine. Then she disappeared again.

Beatriz wished her heart wouldn't race so. She was terrified. What would they do if they caught her?

Sounds of laughter and several voices coming up the stairs. Bill and Mick and Rose and the twins, then the boy and girl, followed by Doris. Everyone looking rather sullen and stuporous except the hosts and the boy and girl.

Bill was his usual jolly self, and Doris was being sarcastic about something—Beatriz couldn't hear what. The boy and girl just looked scared.

Where were Jeanne and Tom? Where was Angela?

An idea Beatriz instantly recognized as daring but very dangerous popped into her head: She would hide downstairs and engineer an escape. Hadn't Mick said that they usually left the keys in the locks? Sure—otherwise he wouldn't have been able to smuggle in that sandwich. She peeked carefully around the end of the log, waiting until Bill and Doris were turned away, then ran on tiptoe to the door and was down the stairs in a moment. A pause at the bottom to listen. Everything quiet.

Making sure to remember the sequence of left and right turns, she explored the maze of corridors, stopping at blind spots to peer around the corner before going on. Everything was the same: variously colored doors nailed to the walls, photographs tacked onto them, and every so often a real doorway. She tried turning the handles of some of these, but they were all locked. And no keys. Not a good sign.

Ah, here was a familiar place—the corridor leading to the room where she and the boy—her father!—had been held. And here, at the end, the key *was* in the lock, and the door opened into the gloom of the room itself.

Empty.

She thought for a moment, then closed the door and ducked into the bathroom. After checking that the door wouldn't automatically lock her in, she pulled it shut it behind her.

Good hiding place. She would stay here until Bill and Doris brought the prisoners back, then she'd release her friends and lead them out. *Let's see . . . two lefts, a right, another left, go through a four-way intersection, one more left, there's the stairs—and we're free!*

She waited for fifteen or twenty minutes, ears straining for any sound, and then had a horrible realization: *They lock the outside door, and Bill has the key! We won't be able to get out! Better leave now before they come back.*

Then it would be on to Plan C, whatever *that* was.

She had just opened the bathroom door to leave when she heard voices approaching. Bill was telling someone that he'd be much happier if he paid more attention to his manners: "We try to be accommodating, but when civility is not returned, well, you see, we have no choice." He was sure that whoever it was would understand and would next time be grateful for the food he was given.

Beatriz quickly pulled the door closed again.

Sound of shuffling feet. Click of a door, turn of the key, and then . . . light flooded the little room as Bill opened the bathroom door. He was alone—Doris was nowhere in sight. "Ah! Good show! What a delightful surprise!"

"I was just leaving." She tried to push past him.

"Sorry. Not possible." He blocked her way. "Missed you, we did. Such a talented guest—one of only a handful any good at riddles!" Beatriz backed away from him, retreating into the bathroom. "Brought me a present, did you?" He eyed the cloth bag. "Let's have a look-see."

He pulled the bag off her shoulder and felt around inside, all the while grinning at Beatriz. At first all he came up with was the bit of cheese, but then he brought out the glass marble in its velvet-lined case. "What's this?" He pulled it out of the case, ignoring the warning label.

"Oh," said Beatriz, casually, "kind of a kaleidoscope thing. It's pretty when it catches the light. . . ."

She hoped "Orb of Immobility" meant what she thought it meant.

"Very nice, very nice." Bill held it up to the light.

After he had gazed into it for a few moments, his mouth slowly opened and his shoulders slumped. He stood very still and started singing softly to himself. "The itsy-bitsy spider went up the . . ." He hesitated. ". . . up the garden spout. Down came the rain, and . . ." His face, which had turned blank and unexpressive, slowly dissolved into a frown. "Down came the rain, and . . ."

"Washed the spider out." said Beatriz quietly.

"Down came the rain, and washed the spider out." A slight smile and a long pause, during which a thin string of drool slipped down from one corner of his mouth.

"Out came the sun," prompted Beatriz.

"Out came the sun and dried up all the rain, and . . ."

Beatriz poked him gently in the stomach, but there was no reaction. She slipped her hand into his pocket, pulled out his keys, and put them in her bag.

He began again. "The itsy-bitsy spider went up the garden spout. . . ."

Tiptoeing to the doorway of the prison cell, she knocked softly. "Rose? You in there?" She unlocked the door. Five pairs of disbelieving eyes stared up at her.

"Shh!" Beatriz put her finger to her lips. "It's me! Are you all here?"

"Man, am I glad to see you!" Rose stumbled briefly as she stood up and swayed a little unsteadily, but she seemed fairly sober. "How did you get here?"

"Long story. Any sign of the witch?"

"Haven't seen her since yesterday."

"Good. Let's get out of here."

"How?"

"I know the way. Just stay with me and don't make any noise. Let's go." She knelt beside Pyramus, who was sitting with his knees up to his chest, looking frightened. "Come on, it'll all be over in a minute. Then we'll be safe." He stood up reluctantly and took his mother's hand. The boy and girl also looked scared but followed her into the corridor.

"What's with him?" Rose pointed at Bill.

". . . and washed the spider out . . ." He was still smiling faintly.

"Why's he singing that?" asked Pyramus.

"Another long story," said Beatriz. "I'll tell you later."

"Out came the sun and dried up all the rain . . ."

They left Bill standing, staring into the glass ball, singing his song and drooling, and cautiously made their way toward the stairs. Some of the corridors were now dark, but most were lit, and it was easy for Beatriz to find the staircase.

Rose stopped them before they went up. "Once we get outside, everybody stay together. We'll walk till we get to the path, not making *any* noise." She glanced at Pyramus. "Once we get there, run like crazy. Run like those little orange guys are nipping at your butts. Okay?"

"Which way?" asked the boy. "On the path, I mean."

Rose thought for a moment. "I guess we'd better head toward Riverrun. I know our witchy girlfriend lives that way, but I don't think there's anything back the other way until you get to town."

"I was at her place yesterday," said Beatriz. "The witch's. And she wasn't there."

"Okay. So we turn left when we get to the path," the boy said.

Everyone nodded, and up they went.

They caught their breath at the top, and Beatriz tried several of Bill's keys in the lock before she found one that worked. After a quick scan of the picnic area, she led them out into a night filled with pale flashes of lightning and low rolls of thunder. The paper lanterns were still glowing, and the remains of dinner lay scattered on the table, and what was that black thing on the other side of—*Oh!*

It was Angela. She turned to face them. She had changed her look to gothic: a black hooded cloak over a gaudy red Victorian camisole and a red velvet skirt. Very witchlike. She was in the middle of clipping her fingernails and registered absolutely no surprise at seeing the runaways. "And where do you think *you're* going?" she asked.

No one spoke.

"Well, you're going *somewhere,* aren't you? Or are you just out for a little after-dinner stroll?"

Still, no one spoke.

"Well, whatever you had in mind, there's been a

change of plans." She pointed a finger at them threateningly.

"Wait," said Beatriz, speaking as calmly as she could. "I know where your book is." *Why did I say that? Because it was the only thing to say to stop her from blasting us.*

The witch paused. "Really? With all my powers I haven't been able to find it. How did *you* manage?"

"I saw it." Beatriz took a deep breath. "Yesterday."

Angela moved around the table and came up to her, standing much too close for comfort. She looked more menacing in her current outfit than she had in the white tights and fuzzy pink sweater.

Beatriz shivered. "I'll tell you if you change them back." She gestured at the boy and girl.

"Oh, you will, will you?" The witch glared at her. "Listen, little girl, I don't make bargains, especially with pipsqueaks like you." She was, as usual, on the verge of losing her temper.

"Oh," said Beatriz. "Well, I guess I won't tell you, then."

"You *will* tell me!"

"I'm sorry. I won't," she said firmly. "Change them back and I'll tell you."

The witch reddened, and although she still spoke calmly, her rising anger was beginning to have an effect on their surroundings. The thunder Beatriz had noticed when they first emerged from underground was getting louder. And there was rustling in the nearby underbrush. Spiky foot-long lizards began skittering through the clearing, rushing in all directions. As the witch stared at Beatriz, the table began vibrating, then shaking, which caused the plates and glasses to dance and a few to fall to the ground.

"Besides, *you're* in no position to make deals of any sort!" Angela pulled the photograph of Beatriz's parents from her cloak. The images now looked only slightly older than the boy and girl. "And I will show you why."

Beatriz didn't answer.

"Who's to be the first? Mommy or Daddy?"

"First? What do you mean 'first'?"

"What do I mean? Watch and find out." Angela raised her voice to be heard over the noise of the thunder that was now roaring almost continuously overhead. One by one the scrambling lizards sprouted sheaths of pale blue fire—already a small section of grass in the clearing was burning. Doris, attracted by the commotion, stood just inside the doorway leading underground, looking on.

"Don't want to choose? Well, Mommy it is, then!" The witch held the photograph up to Beatriz's face and began to tear it, slowly, top to bottom. "It works just . . . like . . . this . . ."

Beatriz watched in horror. Angela was going to rip the image of the girl in half. "No!" she shouted, lunging for the picture.

The witch pulled it away. "Now, now. Didn't your

dinner hosts teach you any manners? I'm sure your *parents* never did."

The witch tore right down to the top of the girl's head. Then, just as she was about to rip through the actual image, a sound like a pistol shot came from the picture, followed by a bright pink spark and a puff of smoke. Angela swore, shook one of her hands, and stuck a burned thumb into her mouth.

She looked confused. The torn photograph began buzzing, softly at first, but quickly rising in volume to a deafening blare.

As the sound reached a peak and then subsided, the image on the paper, which Angela still clung to, began to disappear, leaving a pure white sheet when the noise had faded away completely.

Was that the protection spell? Beatriz wondered. *Did it work?*

Angela wasn't at a loss for long. Acting as if she hadn't been surprised, she said, "It looks like I'll have to use the more traditional method," and raised her wounded hand to point at Beatriz's mother, who was hiding rather ineffectively behind Rose.

Beatriz tried again. "Your book! Don't you want to know where it is? If you do anything to them, I'll never tell you. *Never.* I'll die first! I swear it!"

The witch shook her head and said sarcastically, "Can't change them back without the book."

So it *was* possible to change them back. And if Angela could do it, so could the OSHA people. "Okay, if you won't change them back, at least let them go. Let them go, and I'll tell you." Beatriz held the witch's gaze, unblinking.

For a few moments their eyes locked, and then Angela lowered hers and said, "Oh, all right." She waved the others away. "I'm getting too old for this stuff. Go. Everybody, go!"

Rose stood her ground. "You kids go back to Riverrun—take the boat down to the Fish and Wildlife office and get help," she said. "I'm staying. Go on. Scoot!" She shooed them away.

Pyramus and Thisby, and the boy and the girl, made a wide arc around the witch and left the clearing.

"Okay," said Angela. "Now tell me."

"Do you know," asked Beatriz, "how much trouble you're in?"

"Where's my book?"

"Death is going to be here any minute and he's going to 'process' you. You know what that means, don't you? It isn't too late to—"

"*Where's* my book?"

"You can still save yourself. *Please.* How can anything like that be so important that you'd risk your life for it?"

"You don't know anything about it," Angela said dismissively. "You don't even know who I am." She paused for dramatic effect. "Did you know that we're related? It's true. I'm your aunt. Your uncle M's ex-wife."

Beatriz was stunned. She remembered her parents talking about Uncle M's wife, but she never knew her name and she certainly had no idea Uncle M's wife had been involved in witchcraft, even though Uncle M's bookcase *was* filled with books on magic. Had her parents known?

"Haven't you heard the stories about me? The black sheep of the family? The one with the terrible taste in clothes? 'Oh, look. There's Angela . . . can you *believe* what she's wearing?' I know what they were saying all those years."

Angela continued, sounding like someone who has had to justify her actions to herself over and over. "For nine years your uncle kept me holed up in that horrible New York apartment while he gallivanted all over the globe. It drove me nuts! I wanted to *do* something with my life, not just sit around reading magazines and having lunch with 'the girls.'"

Beatriz stared at her, confused but relieved that the conversation had moved in a new direction; the witch showed no signs of trying to kill anyone at the moment. "But how did you . . . why the . . . ?" she stumbled over her words.

"The books on magic were right there in the apartment! They were *interesting!* I felt important: I was learning something. I was accomplishing something! When he took away *the* book—the only *real* book in the lot—I cried and cried. But he didn't care." She paused. "I just recently discovered that he had sent it to your father to 'protect' me from its—what did he say?—its 'malign influence.' After serving me with divorce papers, he flew off to Hong Kong." Her shoulders slumped. "And now . . ."

She seemed lost in her memories for a moment, then looked up at Beatriz with renewed ferocity. "Where is it?"

Beatriz shook her head. "I don't know," she lied. She couldn't let Angela get her hands on it. "I just said that to save the others. But you've got to stop this, or you're going to die! It can't be worth it!"

Angela reddened again. "Your uncle stole that book from me. It's mine. And if you *do* know where it is— and I have my methods of finding *that* out—*you're* going to be the one to die!" She zipped her forefinger in front of her neck.

Beatriz managed a nervous laugh. "What, like before? Don't you remember the last time you 'killed' me? Death says it isn't my time. He won't *let* me die. He used me to make you do something illegal. Don't you get it?"

"The only thing I get is that you lost my book. *Where is it?*"

"Maybe if you agreed to counseling . . . maybe I could talk to him. . . ."

"Counseling?" Angela looked at Beatriz incredu-lously.

"Well, you said Uncle M drove you crazy."

Rose joined the conversation. "They say these new-fangled antidepressants are really something . . ."

"Antidepressants?" Angela repeated, staring open-mouthed now at both Rose and Beatriz. "I can't believe this." She stood up. "I'm a witch! How can you talk to me about antidepressants?"

"I'm not—" Beatriz began, but Angela raised a hand and pointed at her, as she had pointed at Jim and Leo when she'd turned them into dust. Beatriz stumbled backward, tripping on a root, and fell on the ground. Bill's keys and the photograph she had taken from Angela's cottage spilled out of her shoulder bag.

Grabbing the picture, she held it up in front of her, like a shield. "Stop! This is you, isn't it? When you were young." She made as if to tear it in two.

Angela froze and turned quite pale. "Give that to me," she said, suddenly calm, though her voice was quavering. "Give it to me, and we'll call it even. No need to tell me where the book is—I'll find it eventually. Just give me the photograph and go. Do it now. . . ." She was walking slowly toward Beatriz, who was trying to get up and still keep the picture between herself and the witch. Rose moved to Beatriz's side, facing Angela.

"I don't think I can do that," said Beatriz. "I'm going to keep it. *Stop!*"

Angela stopped, just a few feet away.

"Look out!" cried the witch, looking over Beatriz's shoulder in amazement. In the instant it took Beatriz to break her gaze and turn her head slightly, and before she realized it was a trick, they were struggling for possession of the picture. Beatriz had a good grip on it, but

Angela was terribly strong and nearly pulled it out of her hands.

"No!" cried Beatriz. "It's—"

There was a tearing sound, and each of them fell back clutching half the photograph.

After staring at Beatriz for a moment with a look of absolute horror on her face, the witch clutched at her stomach and groaned.

"I—I—I didn't mean to," cried Beatriz.

"Oh," Angela gasped quietly. "Oh, my." She staggered back, her dark clothes fading to a dingy white in the space of a few seconds. She held up her hands and looked at them. Her skin had turned blood red and was beginning to bubble, as if her body was boiling and blistering from the inside. She fell to the ground in a heap of red and white and, after twitching for a few moments, was still. A small puff of smoke arose from her nostrils.

"Lord, will you look at that," said Rose.

28
REUNION

A HARRUMPHING SOUND came from edge of the clearing, and the black-robed figure of Death walked out from behind a tree, clearing his throat. He glanced at Doris, who disappeared down the stairs.

"That was a very charitable effort on your part—offering to mediate," he said to Beatriz. "I thought I'd wait to see how it came out. You gave it a good shot, but some folks just won't be rehabilitated." He pushed at the lifeless form of Angela with his toe. "She was a lost cause from the beginning."

He snapped his fingers, and the thunder, which had faded to a distant rumble when the witch died, ceased. The last of the lizards, after pausing to look around curiously, ran off into the night, no longer on fire.

Angela's body was beginning to fade in the same way the color had faded from the cat the twins had conjured up. Her clothes became wispy, and soon Beatriz could see the forest floor right through her body. Then she disappeared entirely, leaving behind a smell like burnt toast.

Death continued. "Now, I have a few papers I need you to sign. Is it possible that one of you is a notary? No? Doesn't really matter . . ."

"I've got to find the kids," said Rose, after they had signed three long documents and initialed several more.

"My—my mom and dad." Beatriz was brought back to the sad fact of their enchantment.

Death called out, "Children! You can come back now! Bad lady all gone!" And then, addressing Beatriz, "I had them wait. I think I gave them a bit of a fright, but they were quite obedient. They've been hiding over there, just beyond those trees, quaking in their prover-bial boots."

The four children returned cautiously, as if still expecting something terrible to happen. They formed a semicircle behind Rose.

"Mom?" Beatriz took the girl's hand, again looking into her eyes, as she had at Riverrun. The girl shook her head.

"Mom?" Tears glistened in Beatriz's eyes. Her mother still had no idea who she was.

"Ah," said Death consulting his cell phone, which had just beeped. "I am, as usual, a bit behind schedule, so perhaps you," he looked at Beatriz, "would do the honors? Your dear departed auntie thought she could reset the cosmic clock as though she was switching to daylight-savings time, but nobody gets an extra thirty years, not even best-beloved moms and dads."

He held out two small metal cubes. They were a dull pewtery color, roughly made and imperfectly shaped. Beatriz let the skeletal fingers drop them into her cupped hands, and she gave one to the boy and one to the girl.

Right away she felt something begin to happen.

The air came alive, electrified, with an odor of ozone, the way it smells after a thunderstorm. The nearby trees brightened to a more springlike green, and a soft halo of light blossomed around the hands of the two children holding the cubes. The halo grew brighter and spread up their arms to completely encase their bodies. Through dazzling light Beatriz, shielding her eyes, saw them grow older—taller, wider, and—in her dad's case—hairier. Their faces became sadder, more careworn, but more familiar. In a matter of seconds they were once again the mother and father Beatriz had been searching for.

They had completely burst out of their child-size clothes and stood, nearly naked, like a raggedy Adam and Eve.

"Beatriz!" her mother cried. "What are you . . ." She looked around. "Where *are* we?"

"Get that woman a towel!" said the Grim Reaper. "And an exercise bike for the gentleman!"

Beatriz's father shook his head and looked at her. "Sweetie-pie! What's going on?"

"Mom! Dad!" She grabbed them both in a great tear-filled hug and buried her face between them. The journey that had begun in such loneliness and despair, that had so many times seemed so hopeless, was over. She had thought her parents were gone forever, and now here they were, and everything was going to be just fine. They'd go home, and she'd see her friends and go to the movies and play baseball, and her life would be normal again. Her dad would make her special breakfasts, her mom would drive her to school, and they'd tell her to do her homework and clean up her room, and take her out to dinner on her birthday.

Beatriz's mother was the first to pull away from the hug. "Does anyone have a shirt I could borrow?" She looked around shyly.

Rose took off her jacket and handed it to her. "There you go. I'm Rose. Remember me?"

"Rose? I'm sorry, have we met? I'm Emily."

"'Have we met?' Well, yes and no. But I'm pleased to make your acquaintance in the normal sense. We've been trying to find you for the past week or so, and it turns out you were right under our noses the whole time! Just didn't recognize you."

"We were *what?*" said Harry, wrapping the remains of his shirt around himself.

"Ahem," said Death. "I hate to interrupt this touching scene, but we must get on to part two of my 'Don't Mess with the Program' program." He snapped his bony fingers, and they were all standing in the dining room at Riverrun. "Sorry to rush things along," he continued, "but I've got a date in Baghdad. They *will* not work things out there in a civilized fashion. Very sad. But good for business."

He cleared his throat.

"On to our friends the dust bunnies. Now, where did they get to?" He lifted the bowl Beatriz had used to cover the little pile of ashes. "Ah, there you are." He knelt down beside all that remained of Jim and Leo and Agent Waddle. "Didn't think we'd forget you, did you?"

He pulled back the sleeves of his robe and clapped his long white skeleton hands three times. The men appeared, popping up out of the floor like champagne corks.

"Well, well! A clean sweep," said Jim, looking at his two restored companions. "Caught the floor show, but glad to be back in form, eh, Leo?"

"Floor show! I've had enough of the floor," said Leo. "Thank goodness nobody vacuumed." He pulled a hair out of his mouth. "Yuck."

"Oh, my," said the OSHA agent, patting his pockets for his handkerchief.

If any of them were surprised to see the black figure of Death, they didn't show it.

Beatriz turned to face him. A thought had occurred to her while Jim and Leo were being revived, and the more she had thought about it, the angrier she had become. "Why didn't you just change my mom and dad back the *first* time the witch tried to kill me, if you were going to do it anyway?"

"Good Lord," Death sighed. "Even I need to have a little fun every once in a while. This job gets to be *so* monotonous."

"Oh." Beatriz didn't know what she'd expected him to say, but it certainly wasn't that.

"But you can't say I didn't help you when it counted." Death sounded a bit peeved. "I did make that witch forget her magic voodoo photograph at Señor Borges's inn so you could find it. And I had my fishie friend give you a nudge in the right direction when you needed it. Those are not typically the kinds of things that fall below the radar, so I hope you'll appreciate the risk I took."

"No, no," Beatriz stammered. "I'm grateful. Really."

"Thank you." He seemed mollified. "Now, then. I really must be getting back to work. One last bit of advice: To get here, the deceased created one of her portals on the path back behind this house. I suggest it for your return trip to . . . where was it? Utah? If that doesn't work, try going back to the one near Borges's inn—or click your heels together three times and say something clever."

"And if it doesn't work, you can come and live with us!" said Thisby.

Death's cell phone beeped again. "Must run. Someone's just dying to meet me. Sorry—old joke. See you all again someday—and I am *not* kidding." He whirled around and vanished.

"Eeew! What's that smell?" asked Pyramus.

29
THERE'S NO PLACE LIKE HOME

"CAN ANYONE TELL ME WHAT'S GOING ON?" Beatriz's father asked. "Last I remember, we were in the living room, right, sweetheart? We surprised my brother's ex . . . making off with his sorcery book."

"She did something with it, remember?" said her mother. "Running her hand across one of the pages? I started feeling funny all over."

"And we went out toward the old barn, back in the woods, but we never got there. We ended up here . . . and . . ." Her dad shook his head.

"And I nearly fell down the front steps after taking that horrible book from her." Her mother frowned. "I threw it in the river, and ran away, and then . . . Then I don't know what."

"Must've been the de-aging spell," said Leo. "She brought you here for a few days to let it start to take effect."

"Is there anything to eat?" asked Pyramus.

"Yes, yes. Excellent idea," said Jim. "Leo! What's there to eat? Nothing like being de-moted to work up an appetite. Food first, talk later."

After a raid on the abandoned-clothes chest to find things for Beatriz's parents to wear, and a cursory cleanup of the kitchen, Leo pulled a half-eaten ham from the refrigerator and made everyone sandwiches. There was beer for the grownups (except for Agent

Waddle, who said he was still on duty), milk for the others, and madeleines and ladyfingers for dessert.

Agent Waddle explained that he'd been stationed there a year before to investigate Bill and Doris's slave trade. "Life-force Vampires," he called them.

"The bottom just dropped out of the real estate market when those two moved in. And the witch's nasty little pets didn't help, either. Tourism is *way* down." He sneezed. "But it looks like I can probably make an arrest tomorrow."

They pieced together the story for Beatriz's incredulous parents. Beatriz did most of the talking, helped by Rose and Thisby. Pyramus gave a very long-winded explanation of how he had saved them all when the orange creature attacked them in the forest.

"Goodness! What *are* we going to tell the police?" Beatriz's mother seemed genuinely upset at the prospect of telling a story that no one back home would believe.

After a good deal of discussion, they concluded that a somewhat modified version of the truth would work best. Yes, Uncle M's deranged ex-wife Angela had kidnapped them. They had no idea why, but Uncle M would certainly back them up on the fact that she was . . . unstable. She had taken them somewhere in a car—just a short ride—and kept them tied up in a dark room, in fear for their lives, until finally they managed to untie each other and escape through a window at the back of a house very much like their own. After wandering around in a daze for an hour or so—completely disoriented—they finally found themselves in their own neighborhood, and wouldn't it be a good idea if you officers began looking for Angela right now, before she has a chance to leave town?

They decided Beatriz should say she was just so homesick in New York that she bought a bus ticket with cash she took from Uncle M's "cookie jar" and came back to Iowa, not knowing what she was going to do once she got there.

This all sounded pretty flimsy to Beatriz, but what else were they going to say? "A witch took Mom and Dad to another world, and once I got there, Death helped me find them, and there were these people with wings, and . . ." No. Not going to work.

Agent Waddle finally bowed out, saying he had to find a judge and get a warrant, and that he'd be in touch. He took down addresses and phone numbers from everyone, including Beatriz's parents. (This was a silly thing to do, if he had stopped to think about it—which, being a certain kind of government employee, he didn't.)

The others fell back into a conversation that wandered from one event to another, everyone interrupting everyone else with bits they had forgotten or left out. Leo found more things to eat, and the meal lasted well into the night. The grownups argued about whether or not to go back to the hunter's cabin for the Book of

Spells and finally decided not to. "Let sleeping dogs lie," said Rose. "Besides, it's probably grown feet by now and is running around the forest."

Jim and Leo said they'd take Rose and the twins down the river in the power boat the next day, so they could all meet with the insurance people.

How strange it'll be, thought Beatriz, *back in Des Moines.* Normal life was going to be a bit of an adjustment. *I wonder what Holly would think if I told her what really happened?*

"Ugh." Rose had remembered: "My tax audit!"

"You should have had Mr. Bones write you an excuse." Leo laughed. "Aren't they all part of the same organization anyway?" He pretended to answer a telephone. "Good afternoon! Death and Taxes. How may I direct your call?"

At ten thirty Jim said it was time for bed. He offered to set up cots in the living room, the second story having been so badly damaged during Angela's rampage, but Beatriz said, "Can't we go home now? Please, Dad? Mom?"

Her parents agreed that it would be nice to sleep in their own beds, so Leo found flashlights and they all walked shivering into the cool night air. Pyramus and Thisby, of course, ran ahead. "Hey you kids! Get back here!" called Rose. "I don't want you traipsing off to some alien world or other. I've got enough trouble keeping track of you here."

Holding her parents' hands, Beatriz stopped at the

edge of the forest, awkwardly wondering how to say goodbye.

She hugged Rose. "I don't want to leave you."

"Don't worry, kid, I'll write." Rose laughed. "Sorry. I ain't much at goodbyes. I'll miss you. I'll miss you a lot. Maybe you can drop by sometime."

Beatriz grabbed Pyramus, then Thisby, and gave them each a hug. "You be good. Pay attention to your mom."

"We will . . . we always do. . . . Bye!" and they ran off together through the dark grass, laughing.

"Thank you," she said to Jim and Leo. "I'm sorry about your hotel. And sorry that you got changed into piles of dust."

"Sneak preview," intoned Jim. "The fate of us all. And a good lesson, too: Avoid the Wisterious Stranger."

Wisterious? Does he mean wisteria? Like the vines on the witch's cottage? Beatriz wondered. *Why don't I ever understand what he's talking about?*

"Forget the hotel," said Leo. "Let's take the insurance money and move to the tropics. White-sand beaches. Drinks with little umbrellas. We can even learn to surf."

"At your age?" Jim laughed. "Try something easier, like skydiving."

Beatriz took her parents' hands again, and they walked into the forest. A few yards in, they turned to wave their flashlights and call out a last goodbye. She was sad to be going but couldn't wait to get home to her own bed and her house and her friends.

The path was easy at first, but narrowed after a few minutes, and they had to walk single file.

When was something going to happen? Lights through the trees, ivy on the path, something. Anything.

Ten minutes later Beatriz said, "It can't be this far."

"Maybe just a little more," said her dad.

After another five minutes, they decided to turn back. "We'll try again tomorrow, when we've had a good night's sleep," said her mom, sounding dejected. "Maybe you have to go at a certain time of day, like those ponds you told us about. Or maybe it branched off and we missed it. Anyway . . ."

They stopped and listened to the night. The birch leaves rustled. A bat flitted by. Wind blew across the tops of the pines.

"Your mother's right. We'll try again tomorrow." Her father turned back with an air of resignation, and Beatriz and her mother followed.

Beatriz, disappointed, trailed wearily behind the two adults. It was all she could do to keep awake and concentrate on putting one foot in front of the other. Her parents were talking, but she couldn't make out what they were saying. Something about being abducted by illegal aliens from Mexico?

She couldn't go on much longer; she was falling asleep on her feet. It was a relief when the path widened—they must be getting close to Riverrun. Flat, round stones were set in a row on each side, like a decorative border around a flowerbed. Had she noticed them on the way in?

It was easier to walk here, and that meant she didn't need to concentrate as much, so she was more in danger of dozing off. Once or twice she realized she'd gone several steps with her eyes closed.

How could they just keep going? This was impossible. She had to rest. She would ask them to stop in just a minute. . . .

The stones on the sides of the path were all the same size and spaced one after the other, very regularly. "Are we almost there?" she mumbled.

"Yes, almost there," someone answered.

A minute or so later she realized she had been walking with her eyes closed for quite some time, and she opened them with a start.

She was lying down, staring at a row of small flat stones, perfectly round, sitting on the bookcase beside her bed. She was under her quilt, in her pajamas, in her bed, in her room—in her house.

It was early morning. Everything was quiet.

She got up and tiptoed to her parents' room. The door was open a few inches, and she peeked in to see her mother gently snoring and her father, in his sleep, nudging her and grunting. She went into the living room and looked around. Everything was in its place: The book her dad had been reading to them was on the table next to his chair, her mother's jacket hung on the doorknob where she always left it.

There was mail scattered on the floor, just below the slot in the front door. Bills, ads, and a postcard. A sleepy little town at the edge of a wide green river. She turned it over.

> We miss you, honey. Took the kids into
> the city yesterday and got them each a
> salamander. What next?
>
>   Love,
>   Rose